S0-BYX-450

Beatrice and Virgil

Beatrice and Virgil

A NOVEL

YANN MARTEL

SPIEGEL & GRAU

NEW YORK

2010

AUKITZ

Copyright © 2010 by Yann Martel

Published in the United States by Spiegel & Grau, an imprint of The Random House Publishing Group, a division of Random House, Inc., New York.

SPIEGEL & GRAU and Design is a registered trademark of Random House, Inc.

The excerpts from Gustave Flaubert's "The Legend of Saint Julian Hospitator" were translated from the French by Howard Scott and Phyllis Aronoff.

The illustration on page 142 is by Tomislav Torjanac.

ISBN 978-1-4000-6926-2

Printed in the United States of America

Book design by Caroline Cunningham

Beatrice and Virgil

Henry's second novel, written, like his first, under a pen name, had done well. It had won prizes and was translated into dozens of languages. Henry was invited to book launches and literary festivals around the world; countless schools and book clubs adopted the book; he regularly saw people reading it on planes and trains; Hollywood was set to turn it into a movie; and so on and so forth.

Henry continued to live what was essentially a normal, anonymous life. Writers seldom become public figures. It's their books that rightly hog all the publicity. Readers will easily recognize the cover of a book they've read, but in a café that man over there, is that . . . is that . . . well, it's hard to tell—doesn't he have long hair?—oh, he's gone.

When he was recognized, Henry didn't mind. In his experience, the encounter with a reader was a pleasure. After all, they'd read his book and it had an impact, otherwise why would they come up to him? The meeting had an intimate quality; two strangers were coming together, but to discuss an external matter, a faith object that had moved them both, so all barriers fell. This was no place for lies or bombast.

Voices were quiet; bodies leaned close together; selves were revealed. Sometimes personal confessions were made. One reader told Henry he'd read the novel in prison. Another that she'd read it while battling cancer. A father shared that his family had read it aloud in the aftermath of the premature birth and eventual death of their baby. And there were other such encounters. In each case, an element of his novel—a line, a character, an incident, a symbol—had helped them pull through a crisis in their lives. Some of the readers Henry met became quite emotional. This never failed to affect him and he tried his best to respond in a manner that soothed them.

In the more typical encounters, readers simply wanted to express their appreciation and admiration, now and again accompanied by a material token, a present made or bought: a snapshot, a bookmark, a book. They might have a question or two they hoped to ask, timidly, not meaning to bother. They were grateful for whatever answer he might give. They took the book he signed and held it to their chest with both hands. The bolder ones, usually but not always teenagers, sometimes asked if they could have their picture taken with him. Henry would stand, an arm over their shoulders, smiling at the camera.

Readers walked away, their faces lit up because they'd met him, while his was lit up because he'd met them. Henry had written a novel because there was a hole in him that needed filling, a question that needed answering, a patch of canvas that needed painting—that blend of anxiety, curiosity and joy that is at the origin of art—and he had filled the hole, answered the question, splashed colour on the canvas, all done for himself, because he had to. Then complete strangers told him that his book had filled a hole in them, had answered a question, had brought colour to their lives. The comfort of strangers, be it a smile, a pat on the shoulder or a word of praise, is truly a comfort.

As for fame, fame felt like nothing. Fame was not a sensation like love or hunger or loneliness, welling from within and invisible to the outside eye. It was rather entirely external, coming from the minds of others. It existed in the way people looked at him or behaved towards him. In that, being famous was no different from being gay, or Jewish, or from a visible minority: you are who you are, and then people project onto you some notion they have. Henry was essentially unchanged by the success of his novel. He was the same person he had been before, with the same strengths and the same weaknesses. On the rare occasions when he was approached by a reader in a disagreeable way, he had the last weapon of the writer working under a pseudonym: no, he wasn't XXX, he was just a guy named Henry.

Eventually the business of personally promoting his novel died down, and Henry returned to an existence where he could sit quietly in a room for weeks and months on end. He wrote another book. It involved five years of thinking, researching, writing, and rewriting. The fate of that book is not immaterial to what happened next to Henry, so it bears being described.

The book Henry wrote was in two parts, and he intended them to be published in what the publishing trade calls a flip book: that is, a book with two sets of distinct pages that are attached to a common spine upside down and back-to-back to each other. If you flick your thumb through a flip book, the pages, halfway along, will appear upside down. A head-to-tails flip of the conjoined book will bring you to its fraternal twin. So the name *flip book*.

Henry chose this unusual format because he was concerned with how best to present two literary wares that shared the same title, the same theme, the same concern, but not the same method. He'd in fact written two books: one was a novel, while the other was a piece of nonfiction, an essay. He had taken this double approach because he felt he needed every means at his disposal to tackle his chosen subject. But fiction and nonfiction are very rarely published in the same book. That was the hitch. Tradition holds that the two must be kept apart. That is how our knowledge and impressions of life are sorted in bookstores and libraries—separate aisles, separate floors—and that is how publishers prepare their books, imagination in one package, reason in another. It's not how writers write. A novel is not an entirely unreasonable creation, nor is an essay devoid of imagination. Nor is it how people live. People don't so rigorously separate the imaginative from the rational in their thinking and in their actions. There are truths and there are lies—

these are the transcendent categories, in books as in life. The useful division is between the fiction and nonfiction that speaks the truth and the fiction and nonfiction that utters lies.

Still, the custom, a set way of thinking, posed a problem, Henry realized. If his novel and essay were published separately, as two books, their complementarity would not be so evident and their synergy would likely be lost. They had to be published together. But in what order? The idea of placing the essay before the novel struck Henry as unacceptable. Fiction, being closer to the full experience of life, should take precedence over nonfiction. Stories—individual stories, family stories, national stories—are what stitch together the disparate elements of human existence into a coherent whole. We are story animals. It would not be fitting to place such a grand expression of our being behind a more limited act of exploratory reasoning. But behind serious nonfiction lies the same fact and preoccupation as behind fiction—of being human and what it means—so why should the essay be slotted as an afterword?

Regardless of meritorious status, if novel and essay were published in a sequence in one book, whichever came first would inevitably cast into shadow whichever came second.

Their similarities called for novel and essay to be published together; respect for the rights of each, separately. Hence, after much thinking on Henry's part, the choice of the flip book.

Once he had settled on this format, new advantages leapt

to his mind. The event at the heart of his book was, and still is, profoundly distressing—threw the world upside down, it might be said—so how fitting that the book itself should always be half upside down. Furthermore, if it was published as a flip book, the reader would have to choose in which order to read it. Readers inclined to seek help and reassurance in reason would perhaps read the essay first. Those more comfortable with the more directly emotional approach of fiction might rather start with the novel. Either way, the choice would be the reader's, and empowerment, the possibility of choice, when dealing with upsetting matters, is a good thing. Lastly, there was the detail that a flip book has two front covers. Henry saw more to wraparound jacket art than just added aesthetics. A flip book is a book with two front doors, but no exit. Its form embodies the notion that the matter discussed within has no resolution, no back cover that can be neatly, patly closed on it. Rather, the matter is never finished with; always the reader is brought to a central page where, because the text now appears upside down, the reader is made to understand that he or she has not understood, that he or she *cannot* fully understand, but must think again in a different way and start all over. With this in mind, Henry thought that the two books should end on the same page, with only a blank space between the topsy-turvy texts. Perhaps there could be a simple drawing in that no-man's-land between fiction and nonfiction.

To make things confusing, the term *flip book* also applies

to a novelty item, a small book with a series of slightly changed images or photographs on succeeding pages; when the pages are flicked through quickly, the illusion of animation is created, of a horse galloping and jumping, for example. Later on, Henry had plenty of time to dwell on what cartoon story his flip book would tell if it had been this other type: it would be of a man confidently walking, head high, until he trips and stumbles and falls in a most spectacular fashion.

It should be mentioned, because it is central to the difficulties Henry encountered, to his tripping and stumbling and falling, that his flip book concerned the murder of millions of civilian Jews—men, women, children—by the Nazis and their many willing collaborators in Europe last century, that horrific and protracted outbreak of Jew-hatred that is widely known, by an odd convention that has appropriated a religious term, as the Holocaust. Specifically, Henry's double book was about the ways in which that event was represented in stories. Henry had noticed over years of reading books and watching movies how little actual *fiction* there was about the Holocaust. The take on the event was nearly always historical, factual, documentary, anecdotal, testimonial, literal. The archetypal document on the event was the survivor's memoir, Primo Levi's *If This Is a Man*, for instance. Whereas war—to take another cataclysmic human event—was constantly being turned into something else. War was forever being trivialized, that is, made less than it truly is. Modern wars have killed tens of millions of people and devastated entire countries, yet representations that convey the real nature of war have to jostle to be seen, heard and read amidst the war thrillers, the war comedies, the war romances, the war science fictions, the war propaganda. Yet who thinks of "trivialization" and "war" in the same breath? Has any veterans' group ever made the complaint? No, because that's just how we talk about war, in many ways and for many purposes. With these diverse representations, we come to understand what war means to us.

No such poetic licence was taken with—or given to—the Holocaust. That terrifying event was overwhelmingly represented by a single school: historical realism. The story, always the same story, was always framed by the same dates, set in the same places, featuring the same cast of characters. There were some exceptions. Henry could think of *Maus*, by the American graphic artist Art Spiegelman. David Grossman's *See Under: Love* also took a different approach. But even with these, the peculiar gravity of the event pulled the reader back to the original and literal historical facts. If a story started later or elsewhere, the reader was inevitably marched back in time and across borders to 1943 and to Poland, like the protagonist in Martin Amis's *Time's Arrow*. And so Henry came to wonder: why this suspicion of the imagination, why the resistance to artful metaphor? A work of art works because it is true, not because it is real. Was there not a danger to representing the Holocaust in a way always beholden to factuality? Surely, amidst the texts that related what happened, those vital and necessary diaries, memoirs and histories, there was a spot for the imagination's commentary. Other events in history, including horrifying ones, had been treated by artists, and for the greater good. To take just three well-known instances of artful witness: Orwell with *Animal Farm*, Camus with *The Plague*, Picasso with *Guernica*. In each case the artist had taken a vast, sprawling tragedy, had found its heart, and had represented it in a nonliteral and compact way. The unwieldy encumbrance of history was reduced and packed into a suitcase. Art as suitcase, light, portable, essential—was such a treatment not possible, indeed, was it not necessary, with the greatest tragedy of Europe's Jews?

To exemplify and argue this supplementary way of thinking about the Holocaust, Henry had written his novel and essay. Five years of hard work it had taken him. After he had finished, the dual manuscript was circulated among his various publishers. That's when he was invited to a lunch. Remember the man in the flip book who trips and stumbles and falls. Henry was flown over the Atlantic just for this lunch. It took place in London one spring during the London Book Fair. Henry's editors, four of them, had invited a historian and a bookseller to join them, which Henry took as a sign of double approval, theoretical and commercial. He didn't see at all what was coming. The restaurant was posh, Art Deco in style. Their table, along its two long sides, was gracefully curved, giving it the shape of an eye. A matching curved bench was set into the wall on one side of it. "Why don't you sit there?" one of his editors said, pointing to the middle of the bench. Yes, Henry thought, where else would an author with a new book sit but there, like a bride and groom at the head table. An editor settled on either side of him. Facing them, on four chairs along the opposite curved edge of the table, sat an editor on each side of the historian and the bookseller. Despite the formal setting, it was a cozy arrangement. The waiter brought over the menus and explained the fancy specials of the day. Henry was in high spirits. He thought they were a wedding party.

In fact, they were a firing squad.

In the normal course of things, editors flatter writers into seeing everything that's wrong with their book. Every compliment hides a criticism. It's a diplomatic way to proceed, meant to improve a book without crushing its author's spirit. And so it started, after they had ordered their lunch and small-talked a little, the advance of the complimentary adjectives disguising imperative suggestions, like Birnam Wood moving on Dunsinane Castle. But Henry was a clueless Macbeth. He just wasn't hearing what they were saying. He laughed and waved their increasingly pointed questions aside. He told them, "You're reacting exactly the way readers will—with questions, comments and objections. And that's how it should be. A book is a part of speech. At the heart of mine is an incredibly upsetting event that can survive only in dialogue. So let's talk!"

It was the bookseller, an American bookseller in London, plain-spoken and nasal-sounding, who finally grabbed Henry by the lapels, so to speak, and forced his point upon him clearly and roughly. "Essays are a drag," he said, speaking, Henry supposed, of his retail experience on both sides of the Atlantic but perhaps also of his critical experience reading them. "Especially if you're taking on a sacred cow like the Holocaust. Every few seasons a Holocaust book comes out that bangs on the heart chords"—that's how the bookseller put it—"and goes planetary, but for every one of those there are crates of others that end up being pulped. And with your approach—and I don't just mean the flip book thing—I also mean this idea you have where we're supposed to throw our whole imagination at the Holocaust— Holocaust westerns, Holocaust science fictions, Holocaust Jamaican bobsled team comedies—I mean, where is this going? And then you also want to do it as a *flip book*, which is normally just a gimmick, in the same section as the joke books, and, I don't know, it strikes me that your flip book might just be one big flop book. Flip-flop, flip-flop, flip-flop," he finished, as the first course arrived, an array of tiny dishes with morsels of over-the-top delicacies on them.

"I hear you," Henry replied after blinking a few times and swallowing what felt like a large goldfish, "but we can't always be taking the same approach. Shouldn't the very newness of it, both in the content and in the form, in a *serious* book, attract attention? Won't it be a selling point?"

"Where do you see the book being displayed?" asked the bookseller, as he chewed on his food with an open mouth. "In the fiction section or the nonfiction?"

"Ideally both," Henry replied.

"Not going to happen. Too confusing. Do you know how much stock a bookstore handles? And if we have to worry about turning the book every which way so the right cover is facing out, we'll never see the end of it. And where are you going to put the bar code? It always goes on the back cover. Where do you put a bar code on a book with two front covers?"

"I don't know," said Henry. "On the spine."

"Too narrow."

"On the inside flap."

"Cashiers can't be opening the book up, looking for it everywhere. And what if the book is plastic-wrapped?"

"On a little wraparound band."

"They tear and fall off. And then you don't have a bar code at all—a nightmare."

"I don't know then. I wrote my book on the Holocaust without worrying about where the fucking bar code would go."

"Just trying to help you sell your book," said the book-seller, rolling his eyes.

"What I think Jeff is pointing out," interrupted one of Henry's editors, coming to the rescue, "is that there are certain problems, practical and conceptual, with the book that need to be addressed. For your own good," she emphasized.

Henry tore a piece of bread and furiously swiped at a tapenade made of olives that came from an exclusive grove of six trees in a remote corner of Sicily. He noticed the as-paragus. The waiter had expounded at great length on the sauce, its culinary sophistication, the refinement of its ingredients, on and on. By the sounds of it, one lick of the stuff and you had as good as earned a Ph.D. Henry stabbed an asparagus, wiped it in the pinkish drizzle and stuffed it in his mouth. He was too distracted to taste anything but green mushiness.

"Let's take a different approach," the historian suggested. He had a friendly face and a soothing voice. He tilted his head and peered at Henry over his glasses. "What's your book about?" he asked.

Henry was thrown into confusion. An obvious question, perhaps, but not one that he could answer so easily. That's why people write books, after all, to give full answers to short questions. And the bookseller had rankled him. Henry took a deep breath and collected himself. He tried his best with the historian's question. But his answer came out in stammers and meanders. "My book is about representations of the Holocaust. The event is gone; we are left with stories about it. My book is about a new choice of stories. With a historical event, we not only have to bear witness, that is, tell what happened and address the needs of ghosts. We also have to interpret and conclude, so that the needs of people *today*, the children of ghosts, can be addressed. In addition to the knowledge of history, we need the understanding of art. Stories identify, unify, give meaning to. Just as music is noise that makes sense, a painting is colour that makes sense, so a story is life that makes sense."

"Yes, yes, perhaps," the historian said, brushing Henry's

words aside, staring at him harder, "but what's your book *about*?"

A buzz of nervousness shook Henry on the inside. He tried another tack, to do with the idea behind the flip book. "Fiction and nonfiction are not so easily divided. Fiction may not be real, but it's true; it goes beyond the garland of facts to get to emotional and psychological truths. As for nonfiction, for history, it may be real, but its truth is slippery, hard to access, with no fixed meaning bolted to it. If history doesn't become story, it dies to everyone except the historian. Art is the suitcase of history, carrying the essentials. Art is the life buoy of history. Art is seed, art is memory, art is vaccine." Henry could sense that the historian was about to interrupt him and he hurried along incoherently. "With the Holocaust, we have a tree with massive historical roots and only tiny, scattered fictional fruit. But it's the fruit that holds the seed! It's the fruit that people pick. If there is no fruit, the tree will be forgotten. Each of us is like a flip book," Henry pursued, though it didn't follow from what he was just saying. "Each one of us is a mixture of fact and fiction, a weaving of tales set in our real bodies. Isn't that so?"

"I get all that," the historian said with a trace of impatience. "But once again, *what is your book about*?"

To that third iteration of the question, Henry had no answer. Perhaps he didn't know what his book was about. Perhaps that was the problem with it. His chest rose as he breathed in heavily and sighed. He stared at the white tablecloth, red-faced and at a loss for words.

An editor broke the awkward silence. "Dave has a point," he said. "There needs to be a tighter focus in both the novel and the essay. This book you've written is tremendously powerful, a remarkable achievement, we all agree on that, but as it stands now, the novel lacks drive and the essay lacks unity."

The waiter arrived, Henry's constant saviour during that catastrophic lunch, bringing a new dish, the pretext for a change of topic, forced gaiety and grim eating, until another editor, or the bookseller, or the historian, felt the professional urge—and perhaps the personal one—to take up his or her rifle, take aim at Henry, and shoot again. That was the whole meal, a blundering lurch from the frivolity of over-refined food to the dismemberment of his book, Henry quibbling and squabbling, they reassuring and wrecking, to and fro, back and forth, until there was no more food to eat and nothing left to say. It all came out, wrapped in the kindest words: the novel was tedious, the plot feeble, the characters unconvincing, their fate uninteresting, the point lost; the essay was flimsy, lacking in substance, poorly argued, poorly written. The idea of the flip book was an annoying distraction, besides being commercial suicide. The whole was a complete, unpublishable failure.

When at last lunch ended and he was released, Henry walked out in a daze. Only his legs seemed to be working. They set him off in an unknown direction. After a few minutes he came upon a park. Henry was surprised at what he found there. In Canada, where Henry was from, a park is usually a sanctuary of trees. This London park was not like that. It was an expanse of the loveliest grass, a symphony of green. There were some trees, but they stood very tall with high branches, as if they were mindful of not getting in the way of the unbridled grass. A round pond gleamed in the centre of the park. The weather was warm and sunny and people were out in great numbers. As he wandered about the park, Henry awoke to what had just happened to him. Five years of work had been consigned to oblivion. His mind, stunned into silence, sputtered to life. *I should have said this. . . . I should have said that. . . . Who the fuck was he . . . ? How dare she . . . ?*—so the shouting match in his head went, a full-blown anger fantasy. Henry tried to call his wife, Sarah, in Canada, but she was at work, her cell phone off. He left a rambling, heartbroken message on their voice mail.

A moment came when the tense muscles twitching in Henry's body and the emotions seething inside him came together and spoke in unison: with his fists clenched in the air, he lifted a foot and stamped the ground with all his might, at the same time letting out a choked-up sound from his throat. He hadn't consciously decided to act out like this. It just happened, a snap expression of hurt, fury and frustration. He was near a tree, the soil around it soft and bare, and the impact of his foot-stamping was thunderous, certainly to him, and a couple lying nearby turned his way because of it. Henry stood, amazed. The ground had trembled. He had felt the reverberations. The earth itself had heard him, he thought. He looked up at the tree. It was a giant tree, a galleon with its sails in full rig, an art museum with its entire collection on display, a mosque with a thousand worshippers praising God. He gazed at it for several minutes. A tree had never before been so soothing to him. As he admired it, he could feel the anger and distress draining from him.

Henry looked at the people around him. Lone individuals, couples, families with children, groups; of every race and ethnicity; reading, sleeping, chatting, jogging, playing, walking their dogs—people varied yet at peace with one another. A peacetime park on a sunny day. What need was there to talk about the Holocaust here? If he found some Jews amidst this peaceable gaggle, would they care to have him gore their beautiful day with talk of genocide? Would *anyone* care to have a stranger come up to them whispering, "Hitlerauschwitzsixmillionincandescentsoulsmygodmygodmygod"? And hell, Henry wasn't even Jewish, so why didn't he mind his own business? Everything is context, and clearly the context was wrong. Why write a novel about the Holocaust today? The matter is settled. Primo Levi, Anne Frank and all the others have done it well and for all time. "Let go, let go, let go," Henry intoned. A young man in sandals walked by. *Flip-flop, flip-flop, flip-flop* went his feet, like the bookseller's damning conclusion. "Let go, let go, let go," Henry intoned.

After an hour or so, he made his way to the edge of the park. A sign informed him he was in Hyde Park. The irony struck him. He had entered the park like Mr. Hyde of

Stevenson's tale, deformed by anger, wilfulness and resentment, but he was leaving it more like the good Dr. Jekyll.

Henry realized then what answer he should have given the historian. His flip book was about having his soul ripped out and with it, attached, his tongue. Wasn't that what every Holocaust book was about, aphasia? Henry remembered a statistic: fewer than two percent of Holocaust survivors ever write about or testify to their ordeal. Thus the typical approach of those who do speak about it, so precise and factual, like a stroke victim who's learning how to speak again and who starts with the simplest, clearest syllables. For his part, Henry now joined the vast majority of those who had been shut up by the Holocaust. His flip book was about losing his voice.

And so Henry left Hyde Park no longer a writer. He stopped writing; the urge left him. Was this a case of writer's block? He argued later with Sarah that it wasn't, since a book had been written—two, in fact. It was more accurate to call it writer's abandonment. Henry simply gave up. But if he did not write, he would at least live. A stroll in a London park and an encounter with a beautiful tree at least taught him that useful lesson: if you are pitched into misery, remember that your days on this earth are counted and you might as well make the best of those you have left.

Henry returned to Canada and convinced Sarah they needed a break and a change of scenery. The lure of adventure won her over. In short order, she quit her job, they filled out papers, packed up their things, and moved abroad. They settled in one of those great cities of the world that is a world unto itself, a storied metropolis where all kinds of people find themselves and lose themselves. Perhaps it was New York. Perhaps it was Paris. Perhaps it was Berlin. To that city Henry and Sarah moved because they wanted to live to its pulse for a time. Sarah, who was a nurse, got a work visa and found employment in an addictions clinic. Henry, a resident alien, a rightless ghost, went about filling the parts of his life that were now empty of writing.

He took music lessons, reviving memories (but, alas, few skills) of playing as a teenager. He first tried his hand at the bassoon, but the double reed and the crazy arrangement of the finger holes defeated him. He returned to the clarinet, whose emotional range, from the riotous to the stately, he had not suspected when he was younger. He found a good teacher, an older gentleman, patient, intuitive and funny. The man told Henry that the only native talent needed to play music well was joy. Once, when Henry was labouring on Mozart's clarinet concerto, the teacher interrupted him and said, "Where's the lightness? You've turned Mozart into a heavy, black ox and you're ploughing a field with him." With that, he picked up his own clarinet and produced a burst of music that was so loud, clear and brilliant, a wild storm of gyring notes, that Henry was stunned. It was an aural version of Marc Chagall, with goats, brides, grooms and horses swirling about in a multicoloured sky, a world without gravity. Then the teacher stopped playing, and the sudden emptiness in the room nearly sucked Henry forward. He looked at his own clarinet. The teacher must have seen the expression on Henry's face. "Don't worry," he said. "It's just a question of practice. You'll be there in no time." Henry got back behind his black ox and plodded on. His teacher smiled and closed his eyes and nodded, muttering, "That's nice, that's nice," as if Henry's ox had taken flight.

Again capitalizing on buried youthful knowledge, Henry signed up for Spanish lessons. His mother tongue was French, and the good fortunes of his childhood, his being the son of roving Canadian foreign service officers, had led him to learn English and German with complete fluency. Only Spanish had not fully fit into his brain in those young learning years. He had lived in Costa Rica as a child for three years, but had attended an English school. On the streets of San José, he learned the outer form of Spanish, its colour, but not the canvas that supported it. As a result, his pronunciation and idioms were good, while his grammatical knowledge was not. He sought to remedy this lack by taking lessons with a dreamy Spanish graduate student who was doing a Ph.D. in history.

That Henry had chosen to write in English raised a number of eyebrows in his native land. It was, he explained, *un hasard*. If you go to school in English and in German, you learn to think in English and in German, and then you naturally start to write in English and in German. His first creative scribblings—highly personal efforts never meant to see the light of publication—had been in German, he told bemused journalists. Its crunchy pronunciation, clear phonetic spelling, secret-code grammar and architectural syntax endlessly pleased him. But as he grew more ambitious, he explained, it became patently absurd for a Canadian writer to be writing in German. *Das ist doch verrückt!* He switched to English. Colonialism is a terrible bane for a people upon whom it is imposed, but a blessing for a language. English's drive to exploit the new and the alien, its zeal in robbing words from other languages, its incapacity to feel qualms over the matter, its museum-size overabundance of vocabulary, its shoulder-shrug approach to spelling, its don't-worry-be-happy concern for grammar— the result was a language whose colour and wealth Henry loved. In his entirely personal experience of them, English was jazz music, German was classical music, French was ecclesiastical music, and Spanish was the music from the streets. Which is to say, stab his heart and it would bleed French, slice his brain open and its convolutions would be lined with English and German, and touch his hands and they would feel Spanish. But all this, as an aside.

Henry also joined a respected amateur theatre group. Under an inspired director, the group took its endeavours very seriously. Those were some of Henry's fondest memories of the city, those weeknight rehearsals in which he and his fellow amateur actors slowly brought Pinter and Ibsen and Pirandello and Soyinka to life, leaving their lives at the door and becoming, as best they could, someone else onstage. The fraternity among these dedicated thespians was priceless, and the reaching for emotional heights and depths, for experiences that were vicarious but powerful, was highly instructive in the way great art can be. With each play Henry felt he had lived an extra life, with its attendant portion of wisdom and folly.

After their move, it happened on a few occasions that Henry awoke in the middle of the night, tiptoed out of the bedroom to the computer, and summoned his book onto the screen to wrestle with it. He shortened the essay by half. He hunted down rogue adjectives and adverbs in the novel. He reworked some scenes and sentences over and over. But no matter what he tried, it was still the same doubly flawed book. In a few months, the fruitless urge to revise and resuscitate went away entirely. He even stopped replying to emails from his agent and editors. Sarah suggested gently that he was perhaps depressed. She encouraged him to keep busy. And though this is jumping ahead—and telling an entirely different story—Sarah in time became pregnant and brought into Henry's life a first child, a baby boy, Theo. Beholding him, astounded as he'd never been before, Henry decided that his son would become his pen and by force of being a good, loving father he would write a beautiful life story with him. If Theo was the only pen Henry ever wielded again, so be it.

Still, art is rooted in joy, as his music teacher had pointed out. It was hard after rehearsing a play, or practicing a piece of music, or visiting a museum, or finishing a good book, for Henry not to ache for the access he once had to creative joy.

To keep himself busy, Henry involved himself in a last venture, one that took up more of his daylight hours and in a conventionally more serious way than any other, and this was his work in a café. Actually, it was a *chocolatería*, which is what caught his attention in the first place. Coffee was also served, and it was good coffee too, but The Chocolate Road was primarily a fair-trade cocoa cooperative that produced and retailed chocolate in all its forms, from white to milk to dark, in various degrees of purity and in a wide range of flavours, in bars, boxes and hot-chocolate powders, in addition to cocoa powder and chips for baking. Their name-brand produce came from farm cooperatives in the Dominican Republic, Peru, Paraguay, Costa Rica, and Panama and was sold in an increasing number of health food stores and supermarkets. They were a small but growing business, and their *chocolatería*, which was half chocolate mini-market, half hot-chocolate establishment, was their headquarters. The place had a nice feel to it, with an embossed tin ceiling, rotating art exhibits, good, usually Latin music and a southerly exposure so it was often lit up by sunlight. As it wasn't far from where Henry and Sarah lived, Henry often went there to read his paper and sip on rich hot chocolate.

One day he saw a sign posted in a window: HELP WANTED. On impulse, he inquired. Henry didn't need a job, in fact he couldn't work legally, but he liked the people at The Chocolate Road and he admired their principles. He applied, they were intrigued, they agreed that he would be paid in shares, and, lo, Henry became a small shareholder in a chocolate concern and a part-time waiter and general helper. Sarah was amused and puzzled; she chalked it up to Henry doing research. Quickly his self-consciousness at serving strangers vanished. In fact, he enjoyed being a waiter. It was a moderate form of exercise and it allowed him to observe briefly but constantly the behaviour and dynamics of people, whether solitary drinkers, couples, families, or groups of friends. His hours at The Chocolate Road went by pleasantly.

To complete the picture, Sarah and he adopted a small puppy and a kitten from an animal shelter, neither of them remotely purebred, just bright-eyed and vigorous. The first they named Erasmus, the second Mendelssohn. Henry was curious to see how they would get along. Erasmus proved rambunctious, but easy to train. He often came with Henry on errands. Mendelssohn, a lovely black feline, was a more retiring creature. If strangers visited, she disappeared under the sofa.

That was the life Henry and Sarah constructed for themselves in that great city. They thought they would live there for a year or so, an extended holiday, but they weren't inclined to leave after the first year, nor after the second, and then they stopped thinking about when exactly they would leave.

.   .   .

During their time in the city, Henry's earlier existence as a writer was not entirely forgotten. Reminders gently knocked on the door of his consciousness in the form of letters. By the most roundabout routes, often months after their writers had posted them, he continued to receive letters from readers. A reader in Poland, for example, would write to him care of his publisher in Cracow. After a time, his Polish publisher would forward it to his Canadian literary agent, who would send it on to him. Or a Korean reader would write to him at the address of his British publisher, who would re-expedite the letter, and so on.

Letters came from Great Britain, Canada, the United States, and all other corners of the former British empire, but also from across Europe and Asia, their writers of all ages and stations, the English varying from the confidently refined to the sublimely butchered. Some of those who wrote to him must have felt they were writing a message in a bottle and tossing it into the ocean. But their efforts were not in vain. The solicitous winds and currents of the publishing world steadily brought the letters to Henry.

Some would more accurately be described as packages. They might contain an introductory letter from a high school teacher and a series of earnest essays written by her students about his novel. Or they might contain a photograph or an article that the sender thought might interest Henry. But more typically they were proper letters, typed or handwritten. The typed ones, composed on a computer, were generally more elaborate and discursive, small essays sometimes, while the handwritten ones tended to be shorter and more personal. Henry preferred the latter. He liked the personal art of each writer's handwriting, some nearly robotic in appearance and ultra-legible, others jagged scrawls that nearly defied comprehension. It always astonished him how twenty-six highly conventionalized glyphs could find such varied expression once a living hand set to write them down. Was it Gertrude Stein who said that language was alphabet in disorder? Page layout was another source of interest in handwritten letters, sometimes of concern, as in the cases where the lines of prose were spread over the page like vegetation on ground of uneven quality, spaced out here but bunched up there, often towards the bottom of a page, where the writer was running out of room but still needed to say the essential, hence the sentences that crawled up the side, like the roots of a plant in a too-small pot. Doodles and small drawings were regularly included, art traded for art, his for theirs. Many letters contained questions. A reader had a question, or two, or three.

Henry answered each and every letter. He had a printer make a folded, invitation-size card for him. The front displayed colourful elements from the jacket artwork of various international editions of his book. This card presented two advantages. It was a personal token that the reader might appreciate, and it limited how much Henry could write to a maximum of three small pages: the two inside faces of the card and its back. That allowed for replies long enough to please his readers and short enough to please him.

Why did he reply to so many letters? Because though his novel belonged to his past, it was fresh to every reader who read it and that freshness came through in their letters. To remain silent in the face of kindness and enthusiasm would have been rude. Worse: it would have been thankless. It was gratitude, then, that got Henry into the habit every week of taking the time here and there to sit down and write back to readers. He found he could produce five or so replies without strain wherever he happened to be, in a café or during a lull at The Chocolate Road or at rehearsals.

Henry ignored personal queries, except if the writer was quite young, but he willingly discussed his novel. The questions or comments were often the same. Soon he could reel off standard responses, with easy variations to fit the tone or angle of a particular letter. Henry's novel featured wild animals, and many letters came down to questions about them, about real animals and figurative animals. Readers assumed he had training in zoology, or at the very least a lifelong passion for the natural world. He replied that he had the same broad affection for nature that any sensitive inhabitant of this planet has, but no outstanding interest in animals, no abiding love for them that might be called a character trait. The use of animals in his novel, he explained, was for reasons of craft rather than of sentiment. Speaking before his tribe, naked, he was only human and therefore possibly— likely—surely—a liar. But dressed in furs and feathers, he became a shaman and spoke a greater truth. We are cynical about our own species, but less so about animals, especially wild ones. We might not shelter them from habitat destruction, but we do tend to shelter them from excessive irony.

Henry often used the same lighthearted example in his replies: if I tell a story about a dentist from Bavaria or Saskatchewan, I have to deal with readers' notions about dentists and people from Bavaria or Saskatchewan, those preconceptions and stereotypes that lock people and stories into small boxes. But if it's a *rhinoceros* from Bavaria or Saskatchewan who is the dentist, then it's an entirely different matter. The reader pays closer attention, because he or she has no preconceptions about rhinoceros dentists—from Bavaria or anywhere else. The reader's disbelief begins to lift, like a stage curtain. Now the story can unfold more easily. There's nothing like the unimaginable to make people believe.

Letters came from the postal ether and his replies returned to the postal ether. It was rare that Henry's satchel didn't contain his little author kit: cards, stamps, envelopes and a batch of letters from readers.

And then one winter day Henry received a large envelope from not so far away. It came from within the city, he saw, looking at the return address, but it had travelled the usual circuitous route, in this case via his British publisher. It was clearly from a reader, and one who had much to say, he noted with a sigh, as he felt the thickness of the envelope. He added it to his pile of mail.

He opened it a week later at home. The letter was mostly a photocopy of a short story by Gustave Flaubert, "The Legend of Saint Julian Hospitator". Henry had never heard of it, had only ever read Flaubert's *Madame Bovary*. He was perplexed. He flipped through the story. It was longish and several sections were highlighted in bright yellow. He put it down, wearied at the effort he was being asked to make for a stranger. Perhaps this would be one reader whose letter he would ignore. But while making himself a coffee, he changed his mind. The question niggled at him: why would a reader send him a short story by a nineteenth-century French writer? He went to the study to look up the word *hospitator*. He found it in the full Oxford, the small print bulging under the magnifying glass: "one who receives or entertains hospitably." Well, if he was being invited . . . He sat down at the kitchen table and picked up the story again. It started:

Julian's father and mother lived in a castle on the side of a hill in the middle of the woods.

The four towers at the corners of the castle had pointed roofs with lead cladding, and the foundations of the walls stood on rock outcroppings that fell away steeply to the bottom of the moat.

The stones of the courtyard were as clean as the paving stones in a church. Gargoyles in the form of dragons with their heads facing downward spat the rainwater into the cistern . . .

Within . . . tapestries in the bedchambers gave
protection from the cold . . . cupboards were bursting with
linens . . . cellars piled high with casks of wine . . .

So, a fable set during the Middle Ages. Henry pulled off
the paper clip that held the story together and looked at the
next page. Here was the lord and master:

He would stride through his castle, always wrapped in a
cloak of fox pelts, dispensing justice to his vassals . . .

And here the mother, with the answer to her prayers:

. . . very fair of skin . . . After many prayers, she bore a
son.
. . . great rejoicing . . . a feast that lasted three days and
four nights . . .

He read on:

One night she awoke and saw in a ray of moonlight . . .
the shadowy figure of an old man . . . a hermit . . . without
moving his lips:
"Oh, mother, rejoice, for your son will be a saint!"

Farther down the page, the father also hears a predic-
tion:

. . . was outside the postern gate . . . suddenly a beggar appeared before him . . . a Gypsy . . . stammered these incoherent words:

"Oh! Oh! Your son! . . . Much blood! . . . Much glory! . . . Always blessed by fortune! The family of an emperor."

The son, Julian:

. . . looked like the baby Jesus. He cut his teeth without ever crying.

. . . his mother taught him to sing. To teach him courage, his father lifted him up onto a big horse . . .

A learned old monk taught him the Holy Scriptures . . .

. . . the lord of the castle gave feasts for his old companions in arms . . . they would share memories of the wars they had fought . . . the terrible wounds . . . Julian cried out with delight as he listened to them . . . his father had no doubt that he would one day be a conqueror. But . . . when he came out after the Angelus . . . the bowing paupers . . . would reach into his purse with such modesty . . . his mother truly expected he would one day be an archbishop.

. . . in the chapel . . . no matter how long the service . . . on his knees on his prie-dieu . . . hands joined in prayer.

Henry then came upon an indication of his reader's intent in sending him the story, some paragraphs the reader had neatly and precisely highlighted in yellow concerning young Julian:

One day during mass, he looked up and noticed a little white mouse come out of a hole in the wall. It scurried along the first step to the altar, ran back and forth two or three times, then fled the way it had come. The following Sunday, he was troubled by the thought that he might see the mouse again. It did come back, and every Sunday he would wait for it and would become irritated, until he came to hate it and resolved to rid himself of it.

Having closed the door and sprinkled crumbs of cake on the stairs, he stationed himself in front of the hole with a stick in his hand.

After a very long time, a pink muzzle appeared, followed by the rest of the mouse. He hit it lightly with his stick and was astounded to see the small body lying there motionless. There was a drop of blood on the stone floor. He quickly wiped it up with his sleeve and threw the mouse outside, and said nothing to anyone.

The next page contained another section that was brought to his attention:

One morning as he was walking back along the rampart, he saw a fat pigeon basking in the sun on top of the battlement. Julian stopped to look at it. There was a breach at this place in the castle wall and his hand fell on a broken piece of stone. He swung his arm and the stone hit the bird, which plummeted into the moat.

He scrambled down after it, scratching himself on the underbrush, searching everywhere, more lively than a puppy.

The pigeon, its wings broken, was suspended quivering in the branches of a privet bush.

Its refusal to die irritated the child and he set about to wring its neck. The bird's convulsions made his heart beat faster, filling him with a wild, tumultuous joy. As the bird finally stiffened, he felt faint.

That was the connection, then, in his reader's mind: animals, the killing of. Henry was not shocked. The animals in his novel were not sentimental caricatures. Though used for a literary purpose, they were wild animals, which he attempted to portray with exact behavioural accuracy, and wild animals kill and are killed in a routine way. He intended his story for adults and he allowed himself all the animal violence it required. So a mouse and a pigeon killed by a child exploring the limits of life, getting a feel for death—that was nothing to ruffle him.

He turned the pages. Julian becomes a relentless hunter, with his reader's faithful highlighter as witness:

... preferred to hunt on his own, with his horse and his falcon ... would soon fly back, tearing apart some bird ...
... took herons, kites, crows and vultures in this way.

. . . loved to sound his horn and ride behind his dogs . . . the stag . . . as the dogs tore at its flesh . . .

On misty days . . . go deep into a marsh . . . geese, otters and wild ducks.

. . . slew bears with a knife, bulls with a hatchet and wild boar with a spear . . .

. . . basset hounds . . . rabbits . . . rushed at them . . . broke their backs.

. . . a mountain peak . . . two wild goats . . . approached barefoot . . . plunged a dagger . . .

. . . lake . . . beaver . . . his arrow killed it . . .

Then came a longer section that his reader had marked out:

Then he entered an avenue of tall trees whose tops formed a kind of triumphal arch leading into the forest. A deer leapt out of a thicket, a buck appeared in a clearing, a badger emerged from a hole, a pheasant on the grass spread its tail, and when he had slain them all, more deer appeared, more bucks, more badgers, more pheasants, and blackbirds, jays, ferrets, foxes, hedgehogs, lynx, an infinite variety of animals, more numerous with each step he took. They circled around him, trembling, gazing at him with gentle, pleading eyes. But Julian had not tired of killing, and again and again he drew his crossbow, unsheathed his sword and thrust with his knife, thinking of nothing, remembering nothing. He lived only for the instant, a hunter in an unreal landscape where time had lost all meaning and where everything was happening with dreamlike ease. An extraordinary sight stopped him short: a small valley shaped like an amphitheatre and filled with deer. The animals were huddled together, warming one another with their breath, which hung like a cloud in the surrounding mist.

The prospect of such carnage left him breathless with joy for several minutes. He dismounted, rolled up his sleeves and started to shoot.

At the whistling of the first arrow, all the stags turned their heads in unison. Gaps appeared in their ranks, plaintive cries rose up, and a great agitation ran through the herd.

The lip of the valley was too high for them to cross. The hillsides enclosed them and they leapt about frantically, trying to escape. Julian kept aiming and firing, and the arrows fell like rain. The frantic stags collided, bucked and climbed upon each other; their antlers became entangled and they collapsed together in a writhing mass of flesh.

Finally they all died, stretched out in the sand, their nostrils foaming and their entrails spilling out as the heaving of their bellies gradually subsided. Then all was still.

Night was falling, and beyond the woods, in the space between the branches, the sky was as red as a pool of blood.

Julian leaned against a tree. Wide-eyed, he surveyed the enormity of the massacre, unable to understand how he had managed to do it.

On the other side of the valley, on the edge of the forest, he saw a stag with a doe and a fawn.

The stag was huge and black, with massive antlers and a white beard. The doe, pale as the dead leaves, was grazing the grass, and the spotted fawn trotted along beside her, sucking on a teat.

The crossbow hummed again. The fawn was killed instantly. Its mother, looking up at the sky, gave a deep, heart-rending, almost human cry. Beside himself, Julian shot an arrow straight to her breast and brought her to the ground.

The great stag had seen him and it leapt forward. Julian fired his last arrow at the beast. It pierced its forehead and remained stuck there.

His reader's quoting ended there, so to speak. The neon yellow was turned off and the story left to continue on its own. This was curious, because the very next line mentions that the stag was not killed by Julian's last arrow. The stag rather strides up to him, faces him down, and to the sound of a distant bell breaks into speech and damns him with a curse:

"Accursed! Accursed! Accursed! One day, cruel heart, you will murder your father and your mother!"

This element in the story, surely pivotal, did not seem to arouse the curiosity of his reader.

Henry continued skimming through the story. After hearing the stag's curse, Julian forsakes hunting, leaves his parents and wanders the world. He becomes a mercenary, a very capable one, and much military mayhem ensues, costing the lives of many men from many nations, but winning Julian the affection and gratitude of the Emperor of Occitania, whom he had saved from the Caliph of Cordoba. As a reward, he receives the hand of the emperor's daughter. One of the prophecies about Julian, pronounced to his father, has now come to be: he is of the family of an emperor. But none of this seemed to hold his reader's attention.

One last section was marked in yellow, two paragraphs describing longings simmering below the surface of Julian's otherwise contented conjugal life:

Dressed in crimson, he would stand at a window leaning on his elbows, remembering hunts of years gone by and wishing he could ride across the desert after gazelles and ostriches, lie in wait in the bamboo for leopards, cross forests filled with rhinoceros, climb to the summits of the most inaccessible mountains the better to take aim at eagles, and sail the seas to ice floes to fight the white bears.

Sometimes in a dream he would see himself as our father Adam in the Garden of Eden among all the beasts: by stretching out his arm, he would make them die; or they

would file past him two by two in order of size, from
elephants and lions down to stoats and ducks, like the day
they boarded Noah's ark. From the shadows of a cave, he
would throw javelins at them, never missing his mark;
more animals would come; the slaughter would go on
and on;

Precisely there, at a semicolon, his reader stopped, not
caring to light up the last sentence of the paragraph, short
though it was:

Julian would wake from his dream, his eyes rolling
wildly.

The rest of the story passed without comment, the essential part of it, in fact, how Julian comes to kill his parents, as
predicted by the stag, and, even more importantly, how a life
of sorrow, abnegation and service to others leads him to become the saint announced by the title of the story. No, his
reader stayed with the animals and their bloody fate. Of Julian and his redemption, he seemed to have no interest.

Erasmus was yelping, demanding his walk. Henry had
phone calls to make, lines to work on, a costume that needed
to be found in a vintage clothing store. He put the story
down.

.   .   .

He returned to the story a few days later during an afternoon lull at The Chocolate Road, paying attention to the story as a whole rather than just the parts highlighted by his reader. There was a curious imbalance in the story, with one key element left hanging and unresolved. The dual character of Julian, compassionate yet murderous, made sense in the story's human realm. In his mercenary days, for example, his deeds are violent but they take place within a moral framework. So, "in turn he came to the aid of the Dauphin of France and the King of England, the Knights Templar of Jerusalem, the Surena of the Parthian army, the Negus of Abyssinia and the Emperor of Calicut," and it is implicit that these varied sovereigns deserve his assistance, and thus the need to kill so many enemies. The righteous nature of this spilled blood is made explicit on the same page: "He liberated nations. He rescued queens held captive in towers. It was none other than he who slew the Viper of Milan and the Dragon of Oberbirbach." It is clear that those who oppressed nations and put queens in towers were of the same loathsome ethical stature as the Viper of Milan. The human violence, then, is directed by a moral compass, navigating Julian on a path of lesser evil in which, if there needs to be killing, it is better that those killed be culpable "Scandinavians covered in fish scales . . . Negroes armed with round shields of hippopotamus hide . . . Troglodytes . . . Cannibals," rather than noble dauphins, kings, and Knights Templar of Jerusalem. And this, the use of the compass of morality in times of violence, made sense. Indeed, it is precisely at such times that it must be used.

After Julian kills his parents, slaying them as they sleep in his own bed, mistaking them for his wife and a lover, not knowing that his wife has invited them to rest there, he is keenly aware of the enormity of what he has done. Remorse overwhelms him. His moral compass is spinning.

It is set straight by the end of the story. Julian takes in a horribly disfigured leper who is cold and famished, giving him not only food and shelter, but his own bed, lying naked on top of him—"mouth to mouth, breast to breast"—to give him all the warmth he Christianly can. The leper proves to be Jesus Christ. When the Lord rises in the sky, taking with him the redeemed Julian, what is being represented is the triumph of Julian's blood-spattered moral compass pointing true north. Two modes of seeing the world, one narrative, one religious, are juxtaposed by Flaubert and given their most popular and synonymous conclusions: a happy ending and a sinner saved. All that made sense, fitting the conventions of a traditional hagiography.

But the murder of the animals made no sense. It found no resolution, no reckoning, within the framework of the story, and religiously it fell into an embarrassing void. Julian's pleasure in the pain and extermination of animals—described at greater length and in far more detail than the killing of humans—is only tangentially involved in his damnation and salvation. It is for killing his parents that he wanders the earth forlornly and it is for opening his heart to a divine leper that he is saved. His stupendous hunting carnage only provides the great stag that curses him. Otherwise, the slaughter, a wished-for extinction of animals, is a senseless orgy about which Julian's saviour has not a single word to say. The two of them ascend into eternity, leaving behind quantities of animal blood to dry in silence. This ending seals a reconciliation between Julian and God, but it leaves burning and unredeemed an outrage against animals. This outrage made Flaubert's story memorable, but also, Henry felt, baffling and unsatisfying.

He flipped through the pages one last time. He noticed again how his reader had highlighted in bright yellow every instance of animal massacre, from a single mouse to all the creatures of Eden. That was equally baffling.

The envelope contained more than just the story. Another paper clip held together a second sheaf of pages. It seemed to be an extract from a play, title unknown, author unknown. Henry's guess was that it was the work of his highlighting reader. Lethargy overcame him. He returned Flaubert and the play to their envelope and put it at the bottom of his stack of mail. There was fresh cocoa stock that needed sorting at the back of the store, he remembered.

But over the course of a few weeks, as he dealt with other readers' mail, the envelope reached the top again. One evening Henry was at rehearsal. The theatre where his amateur troupe put on its plays was a former greenhouse for a large horticultural business—hence the name of the company, the Greenhouse Players. A versatile stage had been

built and the rows of shelves for potted plants had been re-
placed by rows of comfortable seats, all thanks to a philanthropist. The precept that location is the key to the success
of a business applies to art, and even to life itself: we thrive
or wither depending on how nourishing our environment
is. This converted greenhouse was a striking setting for a
theatre, allowing one to view the world while walking a
stage (or, more prosaically, to glimpse the cold outdoors
while coddled within the warmth and intimacy of the in-
doors). There Henry was sitting one evening, in front of
a stage and witness to some artful hamming, and it occurred to him that this moment was as good as any to
glance at his Flaubert reader's theatrical effort. He pulled it
out and read.

> (*Virgil and Beatrice are sitting at the foot of the tree.*
> *They are looking out blankly.*
> *Silence.*)

VIRGIL: What I'd give for a pear.

BEATRICE: A pear?

VIRGIL: Yes. A ripe and juicy one.
> (*Pause.*)

BEATRICE: I've never had a pear.

VIRGIL: What?

BEATRICE: In fact, I don't think I've ever set eyes on one.

VIRGIL: How is that possible? It's a common fruit.

BEATRICE: My parents were always eating apples and carrots. I
guess they didn't like pears.

VIRGIL: But pears are so good! I bet you there's a pear tree right around here. (*He looks about.*)

BEATRICE: Describe a pear for me. What is a pear like?

VIRGIL: (*settling back*) I can try. Let's see . . . To start with, a pear has an unusual shape. It's round and fat on the bottom, but tapered on top.

BEATRICE: Like a gourd.

VIRGIL: A *gourd*? You know gourds but you don't know pears? How odd the things we know and don't. At any rate, no, a pear is smaller than an average gourd, and its shape is more pleasing to the eye. A pear becomes tapered in a symmetrical way, its upper half sitting straight and centred atop its lower half. Can you see what I mean?

BEATRICE: I think so.

VIRGIL: Let's start with the bottom half. Can you imagine a fruit that is round and fat?

BEATRICE: Like an apple?

VIRGIL: Not quite. If you look at an apple with your mind's eye, you will notice that the girth of the apple is at its widest either in the middle of the fruit or in the top third, isn't that so?

BEATRICE: You're right. A pear is not like this?

VIRGIL: No. You must imagine an apple that is at its widest in the bottom third.

BEATRICE: I can see it.

VIRGIL: But we must not push the comparison too far. The bottom of a pear is not like an apple's.

BEATRICE: No?

VIRGIL: No. Most apples sit on their buttocks, so to speak, on a circular ridge or on four or five points that keep them from falling over. Past the buttocks, a little ways up, there's what would be the anus of the fruit if the fruit were a beast.

BEATRICE: I see precisely what you mean.

VIRGIL: Well, a pear is not like that. A pear has no buttocks. Its bottom is round.

BEATRICE: So how does it stay up?

VIRGIL: It doesn't. A pear either dangles from a tree or lies on its side.

BEATRICE: As clumsy as an egg.

VIRGIL: There's something else about the bottom of a pear: most pears do not have those vertical grooves that some apples have. Most pears have smooth, round, even bottoms.

BEATRICE: How enchanting.

VIRGIL: It certainly is. Now let us move north past our fruity equator.

BEATRICE: I'm following you.

VIRGIL: There comes this tapering I was telling you about.

BEATRICE: I can't quite see it. Does the fruit come to a point? Is it shaped like a cone?

VIRGIL: No. Imagine the tip of a banana.

BEATRICE: Which tip?

VIRGIL: The end tip, the one you hold in your hand when you're eating one.

BEATRICE: What kind of banana? There are hundreds of
varieties.

VIRGIL: Are there?

BEATRICE: Yes. Some are as small as fat fingers, others are real
clubs. And their shapes vary too, as do their taste.

VIRGIL: I mean the regular, yellow ones that taste really
good.

BEATRICE: The common banana, *M. sapientum*. You probably
have the Gros Michel variety in mind.

VIRGIL: I'm impressed.

BEATRICE: I know bananas.

VIRGIL: Better than a monkey. Take the end tip of a common
banana, then, and place it on top of an apple, taking
into account the differences between apples and
pears that I've just described.

BEATRICE: An interesting graft.

VIRGIL: Now make the lines smoother, gentler. Let the
banana flare out in a friendly way as it merges into
the apple. Can you see it?

BEATRICE: I believe I can.

VIRGIL: One last detail. At the very top of this apple-banana
composite, add a surprisingly tough stalk, a real tree
trunk of a stalk. There, you have an approximation
of a pear.

BEATRICE: A pear sounds like a beautiful fruit.

VIRGIL: It is. In colour, commonly, a pear is yellow with
black spots.

BEATRICE: Like a banana again.

VIRGIL: No, not at all. A pear isn't yellow in so bright, lustreless and opaque a way. It's a paler, translucent yellow, moving towards beige, but not creamy, more watery, approaching the visual texture of a watercolour wash. And the spots are sometimes brown.

BEATRICE: How are the spots distributed?

VIRGIL: Not like the spots on a leopard. It's more a matter of areas of shadowing than of real spots, depending on the degree of maturity of the pear. By the way, a ripe pear bruises easily, so it must be handled with care.

BEATRICE: Of course.

VIRGIL: Now the skin. It's a peculiar skin, the pear's, hard to describe. We were speaking of apples and bananas.

BEATRICE: Yes.

VIRGIL: They have smooth, slippery skins.

BEATRICE: They do.

VIRGIL: A pear does not have so smooth or slippery a skin.

BEATRICE: Really?

VIRGIL: It is so. A pear has a rougher skin.

BEATRICE: Like an avocado's?

VIRGIL: No. But since you mention avocados, a pear is somewhat shaped like an avocado, although the bottom of a pear is usually plumper.

BEATRICE: Fascinating.

VIRGIL: And a pear becomes thinner in its top half in a more pronounced way than an avocado does. Nonetheless, the two fruits are more or less similar in form.

BEATRICE: I see the shape clearly.

VIRGIL: But you cannot compare their skins! An avocado's skin is as warty as a toad's. An avocado looks like a vegetable with leprosy. The pear is characterized by a thin roughness, delicate and interesting to the touch. If you could magnify it a hundred times, do you know what it would sound like, the sound of fingertips running over the skin of a dry pear?

BEATRICE: What?

VIRGIL: It would sound like the diamond of a record player entering a groove. That same dancing crackle, like the burning of the driest, lightest kindling.

BEATRICE: A pear is surely the finest fruit in the world!

VIRGIL: It is, it is! That's the skin of a pear for you.

BEATRICE: Can one eat it?

VIRGIL: Of course. We're not talking here of the waxy, thuggish skin of an orange. The skin of a pear is soft and yielding when ripe.

BEATRICE: And what does a pear taste like?

VIRGIL: Wait. You must smell it first. A ripe pear breathes a fragrance that is watery and subtle, its power lying in the lightness of its impression upon the olfactory sense. Can you imagine the smell of nutmeg or cinnamon?

BEATRICE: I can.

VIRGIL: The smell of a ripe pear has the same effect on the mind as these aromatic spices. The mind is arrested, spellbound, and a thousand and one memories and associations are thrown up as the mind burrows deep to understand the allure of this beguiling smell— which it never comes to understand, by the way.

BEATRICE: But how does it taste? I can't wait any longer.

VIRGIL: A ripe pear overflows with sweet juiciness.

BEATRICE: Oh, that sounds good.

VIRGIL: Slice a pear and you will find that its flesh is incandescent white. It glows with inner light. Those who carry a knife and a pear are never afraid of the dark.

BEATRICE: I must have one.

VIRGIL: The texture of a pear, its consistency, is yet another difficult matter to put into words. Some pears are a little crunchy.

BEATRICE: Like an apple?

VIRGIL: No, not at all like an apple! An apple resists being eaten. An apple is not eaten, it is conquered. The crunchiness of a pear is far more appealing. It is giving and fragile. To eat a pear is akin to . . . kissing.

BEATRICE: Oh, my. It sounds so good.

VIRGIL: The flesh of a pear can be slightly gritty. And yet it melts in the mouth.

BEATRICE: Is such a thing possible?

VIRGIL: With every pear. And that is only the look, the feel, the smell, the texture. I have not even told you of the taste.

BEATRICE: My God!

VIRGIL: The taste of a good pear is such that when you eat one, when your teeth sink into the bliss of one, it becomes a wholly engrossing activity. You want to do nothing else but eat your pear. You would rather sit than stand. You would rather be alone than in company. You would rather have silence than music. All your senses but taste fall inactive. You see nothing, you hear nothing, you feel nothing—or only as it helps you to appreciate the divine taste of your pear.

BEATRICE: But what does it actually taste like?

VIRGIL: A pear tastes like, it tastes like . . . (*He struggles. He gives up with a shrug.*) I don't know. I can't put it into words. A pear tastes like itself.

BEATRICE: (*sadly*) I wish you had a pear.

VIRGIL: And if I had one, I would give it to you. (*Silence.*)

The scene ended with that silence. Henry recognized the names of the characters from Dante, having read *The Divine Comedy* at university, but that didn't help him any. He didn't know what to make of this self-contained playlet; it was a drop whose reflection of the universe was uncertain. He liked the line "Those who carry a knife and a pear are never afraid of the dark." And the cadence was good; he could imagine two actors getting into the scene. But what linked the story of Saint Julian Hospitator and this single-minded, hunger-driven dialogue about an elusive pear escaped him.

Also in the envelope was the following typed note:

```
Dear Sir,
I read your book and much admired it.
I need your help.
                        Yours truly,
```

The signature was barely legible. The second half, symbolizing the last name, was nothing more than a curled line. Henry couldn't make out a single letter or even the number of syllables this scratch might represent. But he could decipher the first name: Henry. Below the careless signing off was an address in the city and a phone number.

His help—what did that mean? What kind of help? From time to time readers sent Henry their writing efforts. Most were no more than proficient, but he wrote encouraging words nonetheless, feeling it was not for him to kill someone's dream. Is that the help this reader wanted: praise, editorial feedback, contacts? Or was it other help? He did receive strange requests on occasion.

He wondered if Henry was a teenager. That might explain the attraction to the blood and guts in the Flaubert story and the lack of interest in the religious theme. But the play was fluidly written, the sentences clean, with no spelling or grammatical mistakes, or syntactical blunders. A bookworm who had a good teacher? With a mother who proudly edited her little budding author? Would a teenager write such a terse note?

Again Henry put the envelope away. Weeks went by this time. Work at The Chocolate Road, two music lessons a week and daily practice, play rehearsals, a burgeoning social life as he and Sarah made friends, the many cultural offerings of a big city, and so on. And Erasmus and Mendelssohn also kept Henry busy. They involved him far more than he expected, Erasmus physically and Mendelssohn philosophically, it might be put, as Henry explored with her the stillness that cats so cultivate, which is to say that when she lay on his lap and he scratched her gently and she started to purr, Henry was reminded of a Buddhist monk meditating to the mantra *Om, Om, Om*, and he fell into idle contemplation himself—and suddenly the day was half over and he had achieved nothing. The solution to this lack of accomplishment was often a long walk with Erasmus. He was a cheerful dog, responsive and forever game. It surprised Henry how much he enjoyed the dog's company. To his embarrassment, he found himself talking to Erasmus not only in the solitude of their apartment, but even during their outings. From the expressions on the dog's face, it seemed he always knew exactly what Henry was talking about.

Still, the envelope glared at Henry from his office table or rebelled in his satchel, unhappily folded in two.

In the end, it was the terseness of the note, so elliptical, and the proximity of the address that persuaded Henry to investigate where his namesake lived. It would be an excuse

for a good walk with Erasmus. He'd write to Henry—
Henry what? Henry examined the envelope. The return address was just that, with no name. No matter: he'd write to
Henry Something on his usual card, thanking him for sharing his creative endeavour with him and wishing him good
luck—with a legible signature at the end of it, but no return
address. *Happening to be here on a visit*, he'd write and he'd
drop it off in his mailbox.

A few days later, Henry wrote to Henry. Of his play he said:

> . . . I found it well constructed and the characters
> interesting. The lightness was engaging and the pacing
> good, delivering an effective scene. You write a good
> pear. I especially liked the line "Those who carry a
> knife . . ." The names of the characters—Virgil and
> Beatrice—intrigued me. Bringing in Dante's *Divine
> Comedy* added an element of depth to my appreciation of
> what you've done. Congratulations. I wish you . . .

Henry wondered if his reader would see through the
meaningless patter of the Dante comment. Of the Flaubert
story, he wrote:

> . . . must thank you for the Flaubert story. I had never
> read "The Legend of Saint Julian Hospitator". You're

right that the hunting descriptions are particularly vivid. So much blood! What can it all mean? . . .

"Sarah, I'm going for a walk. Would you like to come?" Henry asked.

Sarah yawned and shook her head. By then she was healthily, but also sleepily pregnant. Henry put on his coat and set off with Erasmus. The day was brilliantly sunny but cold, hovering only a few degrees above the freezing point.

The walk proved to be longer than Henry had anticipated. He had not properly translated what his eyes saw on the map to the distance their feet would be travelling on the streets. They entered a neighbourhood he didn't know. He looked at the buildings, residential and commercial, noting their changing character, the history of the city and its inhabitants expressing itself architecturally. His lungs breathed in the cool air.

His destination led him to the bum end of an upscale commercial street that featured, among other smart businesses, a grand bridal store, a jeweller, a fancy restaurant and, at the end, on the right side, an attractive café with a large terrace. The terrace was bare of chairs and tables because of the weather, but looming over it on a brick wall, visible from the entrance of the street and promising warmth, was a mural of a cup of coffee with a steaming curl of fragrance wafting from it. At the level of the café, the street turned to the left and then, quickly, to the right. Past this second turn, there was another stretch of businesses on the left side of the street, and, on the right side, the high, windowless brick wall of a large building. A little farther along, the street turned again, to the right this time. The crooked geometry of the street clearly owed to the large building whose rear abutted on it; its imposing size forced the street to make a jog around it. Henry followed along with Erasmus. The businesses on this second part of the street were more modest in character. Henry noticed a dry cleaner, an upholsterer, a small grocery store. He kept an eye on the numbers on the buildings; they were getting close: 1919 . . . 1923 . . . 1929 . . . He turned the corner—and stopped dead in his tracks.

An okapi was looking up the street at him, its head tilted forward and turned his way, as if it were expecting him. Erasmus didn't notice it. He was sniffing at the wall with great interest. Henry pulled him away and crossed the street to get closer. In a large, three-paned bay window, unavoidable and magnificent, was—Henry was tempted to say *lived*—a stuffed okapi set in a diorama of a sultry African jungle. The trees and vines of the diorama leapt out of the bay window onto the surrounding brick wall in an accomplished trompe l'oeil. The animal stood nine feet tall.

The okapi is an odd animal. It has the striped legs of a zebra, the body of a large, reddish-brown antelope, and the head and sloping shoulders of a giraffe, to which it is in fact related. Indeed, once you know the relationship, you can see it: an okapi looks like a short-necked giraffe, with only the striped legs and big, round ears appearing incongruous. It's a peaceable cud-chewer, shy and solitary, that was discovered in the rainforests of the Congo by Europeans only in 1900, though of course it was known to locals before that.

The specimen before Henry was a superlative job. The vitality of its form, the naturalness of its pose, the fine evocation of its habitat—it was remarkable. Here, in an otherwise comprehensively manufactured environment, was a small, brilliant patch of tropical Africa. All it needed was to breathe for the illusion to be reality.

Henry bent down to see if he could find any trace of a stitch along the animal's stomach or legs. There was nothing, only smooth hide flowing over muscles, with here and there ripples of veins. He looked at the eyes; they appeared moist and black. The ears were erect, listening intently. The nose seemed about to tremble. The legs looked ready to bolt. The display had the same testimonial weight as a photograph, the sense that it was an indisputable witness to reality, because when the photograph was taken the photographer necessarily had to *be there*, sharing the same reality. But the act of witness here had an added spatial dimension. That was the nature of the feat Henry was admiring: it was a three-dimensional photograph. In a second, the okapi would bolt, as an okapi in the wild would if it heard the click of a camera.

It was only after some minutes that Henry noticed the street number above the door on the right: 1933. The very address he was looking for! There was a sign in gold letters

on a black background above the bay window: OKAPI TAXI-
DERMY. Henry turned to look in the direction he'd come
from. Craning a bit, he could see the edge of the grocery
store, but otherwise the rest of the street around the corner
was blocked from view. In the other direction, just a few
steps ahead, the street made yet another turn, to the left, to
continue its way now that the big brick building was past.
Okapi Taxidermy was the only business on this hidden
snippet of street. Such an oasis of peace would please an
okapi, but it was surely a graveyard for a business and the
despair of the owner of the store, who would see none of the
busy customer traffic that the main part of the street enjoyed.

A taxidermist. Here was another explanation for the
interest in Saint Julian's hunted animals. Henry didn't hesitate for a moment. His plan had been to drop off his card,
but he had never met a taxidermist before. He didn't even
know taxidermists still existed. Keeping Erasmus on a
tight leash, he pushed the door open and together they entered Okapi Taxidermy. A bell tinkled. He closed the door.
A pane of glass on his left allowed him to continue admiring
the diorama. Henry could now see the okapi from its side
through the twisting vines, as if he were an explorer in a
jungle stealthily coming upon it. How curious the impulses
of natural selection that zebras should warrant getting a
full coat of stripes while okapis only the leggings. Looking
up into the diorama, Henry noticed that among the dis-
creetly placed lights, one light, in a corner above the bay

windows, was set on a mechanism so that it slowly swivelled. In the opposite corner, there was a small fan that also pivoted to-and-fro. He guessed their purpose: in shifting the play of light upon the display, in rustling the leaves ever so gently, an added degree of lifelikeness was created. He looked at the vines closely. He couldn't see the least ridge of plastic or piece of wire or anything to shatter the make-believe. Could they be real? Surely not. Not in this temperate climate, however green a thumb one might have. Perhaps they were real, but somehow preserved, mummified.

"Can I help you?" came a quiet, steady voice.

Henry turned. A tall man was speaking to him. Erasmus growled. Henry yanked on his leash. Before he could say a word, the man said, "Oh, it's you. Just a moment, please," and he disappeared to the side out of sight. *It's you?* Henry wondered if the man had recognized him.

His eyes distracted him from the question. Next to the okapi diorama was a counter with an ancient till upon it, silver in colour and with large, mechanical buttons. Behind the counter, hanging from the wall and from the back of the diorama, were four pale-yellow fibreglass shapes fixed to escutcheon-shaped wooden bases. It took Henry a second to realize what they were: models of heads, the foundations upon which the faces and antlers of hunted animals would be applied. Beneath them, against the wall, were the bit elements of taxidermy: a panel with glass eyeballs of all sizes, diminishing in scale unevenly, going from golf-ball size to marble size in one jump and then shrinking by much finer increments, most of them black, but some coloured and with strange pupils; a board with needles of varying sizes, straight and curving; a rack of small pots of paint; bottles of various liquids, packages of various powders, bags of various stuffing, balls of various thread and twine; some books and magazines concerning taxidermy. These items were set atop and beneath a table that had what appeared to be real zebra legs. Next to the table stood a glass cabinet with an array of insects and colourful butterflies arranged in different display boxes, some featuring a single, spectacular specimen—a large blue butterfly or a beetle that looked like a small rhinoceros—others filled with a number of species, playing on variety.

To the right of the counter, filling the store, was the larger, more striking stock-in-trade of a taxidermist. Three levels of deep, open shelves ran along the walls of the room, and it was a large room with a high ceiling. There were more shelves, free-standing ones, in the middle of the room, also running the length of it. Crammed upon these shelves, each and every one, without any gaps, were animals of all sizes and species, furred and feathered, spotted and scaled, predator and prey. All of them were frozen to the spot, as if Henry's appearance had surprised them and at any moment now they would react—with lightning speed, the way animals do—and the place would break into a pandemonium of snarling and screaming and barking and whining, as on the day Noah's Ark was emptied.

Curiously, Erasmus, the only living animal in the room,

didn't seem struck by all the wild specimens before him. Was it their lack of natural smell? Their uncanny immobility? Whatever the reason, they had no more effect on him than a gallery of dull sculptures and he paid them no attention. With a sigh, he plopped himself onto the floor and rested his head on his paws, as bored as a child in an art museum.

Henry, on the other hand, stared wide-eyed. A tingle of excitement passed through him. Now here was a stage full of stories. He took in a set of three tigers standing in the middle of the room. A male was crouching, staring dead ahead, ears swivelled around, every hair bristling. A female stood a little behind him, a paw raised in the air, a snarl upon her face, her tail anxiously curled in the air. Lastly, a cub had his head turned to one side, distracted momentarily, but he too was apprehensive, his claws drawn. The nervous tension emanating from the trio was palpable, electric. In a second, instinct would take over and the situation would come to a head. The male would confront—what? whom? A rogue male who had just appeared? There would be fearsome roars, perhaps outright combat if each male felt he could not back down. The female would turn and instantly vanish, leaping through the vegetation, moving all the faster to encourage her cub to keep up. The cub would not slacken in his efforts, no matter the pounding of his heart. Only the knowledge that these animals were dead, certainly dead, kept an equally fearful reaction from overtaking Henry. But his heart was pounding.

He looked at the rest of the room. There was no natural light except that which filtered through the diorama and the front door's pane of glass, and the artificial lighting hanging from the ceiling was not strong. Shadows manufactured environments: forests, rocks, branches. At a glance, close at hand, Henry could see shrews, mice, hamsters, guinea pigs, rats, a domestic cat, a hedgehog, cottontail rabbits, two bats (one in flight, one upside down, hanging from a shelf), a mink, a weasel, a hare, a platypus, an iguana, a kiwi bird, a red squirrel, a grey fox, a badger, an armadillo, a beaver, an otter, a raccoon, a skunk, a lemur, a wallaby, a koala, a king penguin, an aardvark. Grouped together were some snakes, among them a skinny, bright green one, a reared-up cobra, its hood expanded, and a boa with a fat coil overhanging the shelf. Farther along he could make out a capybara, a lynx, a porcupine, a mouflon sheep with incredible horns, a wolf, a leopard, a tapir, a lion, a gazelle of some kind, a seal, a cheetah, a baboon, a chimpanzee. Along part of one shelf were whole mounted skeletons of mid-size four-legged animals, five or six of them, next to which was a skull set on a rod under a glass dome. At the far end of the room appeared a gnu, an oryx antelope, an ostrich, a grizzly bear standing high on its rear legs, and a baby hippopotamus with a peacock in full display resting atop it. Packing the upper shelves were concerts of birds, splashes of colour: hummingbirds, parrots, jays and magpies, ducks and pheasants, hawks and owls, a toucan, three small penguins, a Canada goose, a turkey and others Henry couldn't identify, some of these birds perched, others about to take off, and still others in full flight, suspended from the ceiling, obscuring it. At the very back of the room, above the animals on the floor, animal heads—lions, tigers, several types of deer, a moose, a camel, a giraffe, an Indian elephant—covered the wall, giving the impression that the room was the end of a tunnel filled with animals and shadows.

Aside from the koala sitting next to the wallaby and the jaguar next to the tapir and a few other elementary pairings, there was minimal sense to how the animals were ordered. The winged were generally above the footed and the smaller above the larger, with the very large tending to crowd the back of the room. Beyond that, anything went. Strangely, this higgledy-piggledy arrangement, by dispensing with notions of distinction and grouping, created an overall impression of unity, a shared culture of animalness. Here, diverse but one, linked by a common bond, was a community.

"I have your book here," said the man, emerging from a side door.

The man had recognized Henry. He had a sharp eye. Henry hadn't done much media in years and the man's memory of his appearance couldn't be a fresh one.

"And I have a card for you," Henry said automatically, though he had not meant to deliver it in person. "Would you like me to sign your book?"

"If you want."

"A pleasure meeting you," said Henry, extending his hand.

"Oh, yes." The shopkeeper's soft hand enveloped Henry's. They exchanged items. Henry inscribed the book. He wrote the first thing that came to his mind: *To Henry, a friend of animals.* The man, meanwhile, opened the envelope and took a long time to read the card. Henry worried about what he had written. But it gave him time to observe the man. He was tall, well over six feet, with a wide, gaunt body, his clothes hanging from big bones. His arms were long, his hands large. His black hair was oiled and combed back, to be forgotten, and under a tall forehead he had a pale, flat, long-nosed, jowly face. He looked to be in his sixties. His expression was serious, the eyebrows knitted, the dark eyes staring. He didn't seem a naturally social being. The handshake had been awkward, apparently not a grace practiced often, and the signing of the book had plainly been Henry's idea, not his.

Erasmus seemed intrigued by the man, although not in his usual over-friendly way. He got to his feet and inched forward, sniffing tentatively at the hem of the man's trousers, his legs spread out and tense, ready to scurry away should he smell anything alarming. Seeing that the man wasn't reacting with a smile or a greeting or even a glance in the usual way of people who are meeting a friendly dog, Henry tugged on Erasmus's leash and brought him back to him. Inexplicably, Henry was feeling nervous.

"Is the dog a problem? I can easily tie him outside," he said.

"No," the man replied, without lifting his eyes from the card.

"You can ignore the card. I just wrote it quickly, in case I didn't find you."

"That's fine." He closed the card and placed it in the book Henry had returned to him. He did not look to see what Henry had written in the book, nor did he have anything to say about what he had written in the card.

"Is this your store?" Henry asked.

"It is," replied the man.

"An amazing place. I've never seen anything like it. How long have you been a taxidermist?"

"Over sixty-five years. I started when I was sixteen and I've never stopped."

Henry was taken aback. Over sixty-five years? The man must be in his early eighties, then. He certainly didn't look it.

"These tigers are remarkable."

"The female and the cub I was given by Van Ingen and Van Ingen, a firm in India, when they closed. The male is my work, from a zoo. He died of a heart defect."

He spoke without the least hesitation, and his delivery was clear and certain. He was not afraid of silence, either. I don't speak like that, Henry thought. I speak both quickly and haltingly, in stumbles and incomplete sentences that trail off.

"And all these animals are for sale?"

"Nearly all. A few are museum items I've repaired that are drying. A small number are display items. The okapi is not for sale, nor is the platypus or the aardvark. But the rest, yes, they're for sale."

"Do you mind if I have a look?"

"Go ahead. Look as closely as you want. All the animals are alive—it's time that has stopped."

Pulling Erasmus along, Henry started going around the store. The taxidermist stayed in place, silent and staring. Henry discovered that behind most animals others were hiding, often of the same kind, but not always. A colony of tortoises was tucked under the legs of the cheetah. Next to the mouflon sheep, on the floor, was a pile of antlers. Rolled-up hides stood in the back corner next to the ostrich, along with some tusks and horns. Some fish mounted on wooden boards—trout and bass, a puffer fish—lay at the feet of the bear. The craftsmanship was superlative. The fur, the scales, the plumage—they positively glistened with life. Henry felt that if he stamped a foot, all these creatures would jump and flee. And despite being so packed together, each animal had its own expression, its own personal situation, its own story. Henry wondered if he would find here the stag that had cursed Saint Julian Hospitator. Or perhaps the bears slain with a knife, the bulls with a hatchet, the beaver in the lake with an arrow?

The elephant's trunk was within touching distance. A shiny drop was forming from one of its nostrils, as if the animal had just had a good, wet sneeze. Henry felt like reaching up to touch the drop. But he knew—his mind told him—that all he would feel would be a hard drop of clear synthetic resin.

"People just come in and buy the animals off the shelf?" he asked.

"Some."

"I suppose hunters bring you animals?"

"That too."

"I see."

The man was no good at small talk. Henry crouched and parked his stare on a wolf and waited. It was the taxidermist's turn to make an effort, he decided. Henry had come to him, after all, had walked all that way, and the man was wanting his help, he had claimed. And Henry was quite happy just to keep on looking. The wolf in front of him was in a running motion, its front legs lifted in the air, reaching for the ground ahead of it. The shoulders were hunched, the most expressive part of the animal's unstoppable forward surge. The right rear leg, having just pushed off, was now pointing straight back. So the whole animal was supported in the air in a completely natural pose by a single rear leg. Another wolf was standing against the wall, tall and still, its head turned to one side, observing something in the distance with idle curiosity, a picture of perfect animal poise.

"So, why don't you tell me a little about Okapi Taxidermy," Henry finally said.

That did it. He had touched on the right subject. The taxidermist delivered a speech. "At Okapi Taxidermy, we are professional natural-history preparators. Skins, heads, horns, hooves, trophies, rugs, natural-history specimens in every kind of mount, head to whole, we are experts not only in taxidermy but in osteology, that is, the treating and mounting of skulls, bones, and articulated skeletons. We are also masters in all the techniques and materials needed to build any habitat setting you might desire in which to display your mounted animal, from the simplest branch to the most complex diorama. We make mannequins of every kind for amateur taxidermists who might wish to mount a favourite or memorable animal on their own. We can also manufacture any kind of ornament or furniture made from animal parts. We supply every taxidermic need, from paint for fish mounts to eyes of all kinds to tools and padding and needles and threads and wood bases, to more specialized needs for natural-history dioramas. We custom-make display cases of all shapes and sizes, for mammals, birds, fish, and skeletons. We provide mechanical hares for greyhound races. We can preserve the cycle of life for you, whether the embryonic development of chicks or the life cycle of frogs or butterflies, real and preserved, or enlarged in plaster, if you wish. We can also make models of animals that interrupt the cycle of life: fleas, tsetse flies, common flies, mosquitoes, and the like. We are skilled at packing and crating any taxidermic work so that it will arrive at its destination safe and sound. We sell, but we also rent mounted specimens. We fix. We attend to what is dirty, dusty, discoloured, damaged, broken, shrunken, chipped, shorn, worn, torn, fallen in, fallen out, missing, afflicted by insects. We clean and dust—dust is the eternal enemy of the taxidermist. We sew back. We comb and brush. We oil antlers and polish tusks and ivory. We repaint and shellac fish. We repair and renew habitat groups and dioramas. There is no detail we overlook. We guarantee everything we do and provide complete after-sale care at a reasonable charge. We are a reputable firm with a long list of satisfied customers, from the most discerning individuals to the most demanding institutions. We are, in a word, a complete, one-stop taxidermy shop."

All said in one go, effortlessly, his arms at his sides, with no tics or twitches to distract, like an actor on a stage. He would do well in his amateur theatre group, Henry thought. He noted the repeated use of *we*. He wondered if the plural pronoun behind Okapi Taxidermy—we are, we make, we do—was the small-business equivalent of the royal we, meant to create an impression grander, more convincing, than a lonely old man who still had to work for a living.

"That's very impressive. How's business?"

"It's dying. The taxidermy business is a dying business, has been for years, like the materials we work with. No one wants animals anymore, except for a handful of token domesticated species. The wild ones, the real ones, they're all going, if not already gone."

At that moment, listening to his tone of voice and observing the set of his face, Henry got a clue about the man, an insight into his personality: he had no sense of humour, no cheerfulness. He was as serious and sober as a microscope. Henry's nervousness left him. That would be how he would deal with the man: he would stay on his solemn level. Henry wondered about the play the taxidermist had sent him. The contrast couldn't be greater between this over-serious giant and a bantering dialogue about a pear. But sometimes art comes from a secret self. Perhaps all his lightness went into his writing, leaving him drained of it in person. Henry suspected that what he was seeing was the taxidermist's public face.

"I'm sorry to hear that. It's clearly a business you love."

The taxidermist made no reply. Henry looked around. An impulse of pity made him think he should buy a stuffed animal. He had noticed the platypus, tucked away on a shelf, but it wasn't for sale. It was appealingly mounted on a dark wood base, floating two inches above it, webbed feet outstretched, as if the strange little animal were swimming along a riverbed. Henry wanted to touch its bill but refrained. Among the displays of skeletons, there was a remarkable skull. Hovering under a glass dome at the end of a golden rod, it had the appearance of a holy relic. The bones shone bright white, and there was power to that whiteness, as there was to the stare of the large eyeball sockets. Henry made his way back to the front of the store, Erasmus at his side.

"How much are the tigers, out of curiosity?" he asked.

The taxidermist moved to the counter, pulled open a drawer and brought out a notebook. He flipped through some pages.

"The female and the cub, as I said, are from Van Ingen and Van Ingen. In addition to being fine specimens, superbly mounted, they're also antiques. Together with the male, that would be . . ." The taxidermist cited a figure.

Henry whistled in his head. At that price, if those animals had wheels, they'd be a sports car.

"And the cheetah?"

The notebook was again consulted. "It sells for . . ." and the taxidermist stated another figure.

Two wheels this time: a sleek, powerful motorcycle.

Henry looked at a few more animals.

"This is all fascinating. I'm glad I came. But I don't want to keep you any longer."

"Wait."

Henry froze. He wondered if all the animals had also tensed.

"Yes?"

"I need your help," the taxidermist said.

"Ah, yes. My help. You mentioned that in your letter. What exactly did you have in mind?"

Henry wondered if the man was going to make him a business proposition. He had invested small sums here and there, mostly in ventures that had failed. Was he now going to find himself investing in a taxidermy concern? The thought intrigued him. He rather liked the idea of being involved with all these animals.

"Please come to my workshop," the taxidermist said, signalling with his wide hand the side door through which he had gone to fetch Henry's book. There was something commanding about the gesture.

"Sure," said Henry, and he walked through.

The workshop was smaller than the showroom, but better lit. A barred window cut across the back wall above a double door, letting in natural light. A faint smell of chemicals hung in the air. Henry noticed things quickly. A large, deep sink. A shelf with a row of books. Some sturdy worktables and counters. The materials of the taxidermy trade: jars of chemical products; bottles of glue; a box of short iron rods; a large cardboard box of cotton batting; spools of thread and wire; a hefty plastic bag of clay; pieces and planks of wood. Neatly arranged tools lay on the tables, among them surgical scalpels; knives and scissors; pliers and pincers; boxes of tacks and nails; a measuring tape; hammers and mallets; saws and hacksaws; a file; chisels; clamps; modeling tools; small paintbrushes. A chain was hanging from the wall with a hook at the end of it. There were animals again, on shelves and on the floor, though far fewer than in the display room, and some were entirely disembodied, just a pile of hide or a mound of feathers, and others were works-in-progress. A mannequin made of wood, wire, and cotton batting for a round animal, a large bird likely, lay unfinished on a worktable. At the moment, the taxidermist appeared to be working on a deer head mount. The skin was not yet properly fitted on the fibreglass mannequin head and the mouth was a tongueless, toothless gaping hole revealing the yellow fibreglass jaw of the mannequin. The eyes had that same yellow glow. It looked grotesquely unnatural, a cervine version of Frankenstein.

A desk stood in the corner of the room opposite the door. On top of it, among various papers and items, Henry noticed a dictionary and an old electric typewriter—the taxidermist apparently had no interest in new technologies. The desk had one wooden chair. The taxidermist sat in it.

"Please," he said. He indicated the only other place to sit, a plain stool in front of the desk. Without worrying any further about Henry's comfort, he pulled a cassette player from a drawer. Henry sat down. The taxidermist set the player on the desk and pressed the rewind button. There was a whirr, a blocking sound, a moment of strain, then the rewind button popped up. He pressed the play button. "Listen closely," he said.

At first, Henry could hear only a grainy sound as an old tape rubbed against a tired head. Then another sound emerged, at first distant, then coming through in waves with greater clarity. It was a clamouring chorus of barked grunts. These went on for some several seconds until suddenly, from their midst, drowning them out, a new and distinctive shout erupted. It was loud and continuous, a robust howl that kept increasing in volume until it reached a prolonged and formidable roaring pitch, vaguely like someone waking up and stretching and letting off a mighty growl, only someone superhuman—Nimrod, a Titan, Hercules. It had a deep, throaty timbre, and it was very powerful. Henry had never heard anything like it. What emotion did it express? Fear? Anger? Lament? He couldn't tell.

Erasmus seemed to know. As soon as he heard the barked grunts he stiffened and his ears pricked up. Henry thought it was plain curiosity. But the dog seemed to be trembling. When the howl started, he burst into barking. He too was either afraid or angry. Henry bent down and picked Erasmus up and squeezed him to his chest to silence him.

"I'm sorry," he said to the taxidermist. "I'll just be a second." He hurried to the showroom and tied Erasmus to the leg of the till counter. *"Shhh!"* he said to the dog. He returned to the shop.

"What was that?" he asked, sitting on the stool again and pointing at the cassette player.

"It's Virgil," replied the taxidermist.

"Who?"

"They're both here."

He indicated what he meant with a nod of the head. In front of his desk, set next to the wall, stood a stuffed donkey with a stuffed monkey sitting on its back.

"Beatrice and Virgil? From the play you sent me?" Henry asked.

"Yes. They were alive once."

"You wrote that?"

"Yes. What I sent you is the opening scene."

"The two characters are *animals*?"

"That's right, like in your novel. Beatrice is the donkey, Virgil is the monkey."

So he *was* the author of the play after all. A play featuring two animals that have an extended conversation about a pear. Henry was surprised. He would have picked realism as the taxidermist's favoured style of representation. Evidently he was misjudging him. Henry looked at the dramatis personae standing next to him. They were exceptionally lifelike.

"Why a monkey and a donkey?" he asked.

"The howler monkey was collected by a scientific team in Bolivia. It died in transit. The donkey came from a petting zoo. It was hit by a delivery truck. A church was thinking of using it for a nativity scene. Both animals happened to arrive on the same day at my shop. I had never prepared a donkey before, nor a howler. But the church changed its mind and the scientific institute decided it didn't need the howler. I kept the deposits and the animals. That happened on the same day too, their abandonment, and the two animals came together in my mind. I finished preparing them, but I've never displayed them and they're not for sale. I've had them for some thirty years now. Virgil and Beatrice— my guides through hell."

Hell? What hell? Henry wondered. But at least now he understood the connection to *The Divine Comedy*. Dante is guided through inferno and purgatory by Virgil and then through paradise by Beatrice. And what would be more natural for a taxidermist with literary aspirations than to fashion his characters out of what he worked with every day? So of course he would use talking animals.

Henry noticed three pieces of paper taped to the wall next to the two animals. On each was text surrounded by a border:

FELLOW CITIZENS!
_____

Large monkey of surly disposition.

Eyes, voice, tail and gait indicative of

cunning temperament. Clings to life tenaciously.

Characterized by antisocial behaviour.

Ugly.
_____

BEWARE!
_____

Large prehensile-tailed monkey

with grotesque jaw, often with attempt at

concealment by means of jowl beard.

Slothful and heavy-looking.

Scowling countenance. Unbearable voice.

Untrustworthy.
_____

```
                    ATTENTION!
                   ─────────────

            Large monkey with black face

        and bearded chin. Body thick and heavy.

            Tail long and naked at tip.

          Movements sluggish and deliberate.

         Cry powerful, harsh, insufferable.

            Temperamentally undesirable.

              Disposed to dishonesty.
        ─────────────────────────────────────
```

"Are these part of your play?" Henry asked.

"Yes. They're posters. I have a scene where they would be projected onto the back wall as Beatrice is talking."

Henry read the posters again. "The monkey isn't popular, is he?" he asked.

"No, not at all," replied the taxidermist. "Let me show you the scene."

He started going through some papers on his desk. Without hesitation he had taken Henry's answer to be yes. Henry didn't mind. Beyond indulging the man out of politeness, he was intrigued.

"Here it is."

Henry extended his hand to take the papers. The taxidermist left Henry's hand hanging in the air and cleared his throat instead. Henry realized he was intending to read the scene aloud to him. After looking at the text for a moment, the taxidermist started:

VIRGIL: Why don't we look for something to eat? I found a banana. We might find something else.

BEATRICE: That's an idea.

VIRGIL: Let's have a look around. Why don't you go that way, and I'll go this way, and we'll meet back here in a few minutes.

BEATRICE: (*with hesitation*) All right.

Food again, thought Henry. First a pear, now a banana. The man is obsessed with food.

(*Virgil scampers off to the right, while Beatrice clops off to the left.*
A short while later. Beatrice is back first. She looks worried. She inspects the tree, to assure herself that it's the same one as before and that she's back in the right spot.)

BEATRICE: (*looking to the right*) Virgil. VIIIIIIIRGIL!
(*No reply.*)

BEATRICE: (*looking to the left*) VIRGIL, WHERE ARE YOU?
(*No reply. Beatrice looks miserable. She has no choice but to wait. She frets. Long pause.*)

BEATRICE: (*to the right*) VIIIIIIIRGIL! (*to the left*) VIIIIIIIRGIL!
(*Still no reply.*)

BEATRICE: (*pretending to be talking to someone*) Excuse me, have you seen . . . Yes, he's a red howler monkey . . . Yes, yes, like the ones you've read about, but those posters are all lies . . . No, I tell you, he's the sweetest, kindest, most honourable animal . . . That's right, an *Alouatta seniculus sara*, if you want to be taxonomically precise, but who invented that science, I ask you? What do these terms mean? And do they really matter? They're nonsense, gibberish.

The taxidermist broke off his reading. "That's when the projector would be turned on and the posters would appear side by side in big letters on the back wall."

He returned to his play. He read in a steady, unaffected voice, laying out the words in an easy way. To each character he gave a different tone, so Beatrice the donkey spoke softly while Virgil the monkey expressed himself with greater animation. Henry found himself listening to them without being aware of listening to the taxidermist.

BEATRICE: (*still talking to an imaginary interlocutor*) Such outrages I have read. They're impossible to avoid. Posters, newspaper articles, pamphlets, books—their poison finds its way into people's hearts and minds and from there onto their tongues. Yet they have nothing to do with truth or reality. The red howler in question—he has a name, you know. His name is Virgil. Virgil is the most handsome animal. He has—

The taxidermist stopped again and looked up at Henry. He seemed to hesitate. "Well, how would you describe Virgil? What does he look like to you?" He got up abruptly and went to one of the workbenches. He brought over a powerful lamp. "Here, I have a light," he said, with resolve. He set it on the desk and directed its beam at the monkey. Then he waited.

It took Henry a moment to realize that the man was serious. He really did want him to describe the stuffed monkey. It dawned on Henry with amazement: *this is the help he wants*. It's not a matter of encouragement, or confession, or connections. The help he wants is with words. Had the taxidermist made the request to Henry ahead of time in his letter, he would have refused, as he had refused writing commissions of all kinds for years. But here, in this setting, next to the very characters, in the fire of the moment, something in Henry woke up and yearned to rise to the challenge.

"What does he look like to me?" Henry said. The taxidermist nodded. Henry leaned close to the animal, to Virgil, since he had a name. He felt like a doctor about to examine a patient. He noticed that Virgil was not sitting on the donkey, on Beatrice, the way the peacock in the other room was set on the hippopotamus, as a convenience in the absence of a table. He had rather been mounted so that he sat naturally on Beatrice. His rump, two legs and an outstretched arm were laid out in a way that fitted the shape of her back perfectly, and his long tail, curled at its end, flowed so that it rested snugly against her back and side, looking very much like a casually set anchor in case she made a sudden movement. His other arm was resting on a bent knee, hand open, palm up, in a relaxed pose. Virgil had his mouth open and Beatrice her head partly turned and one ear swivelled round. He was saying something and she was listening. . . .

Henry thought for a moment. Then he started. "Off the top of my head, without any preparation or much thought, I'd say Virgil has the pleasing dimensions of a smaller dog, neither too bulky nor too slight. I'd say he has a handsome head, with a short snout, luminous reddish-brown eyes, small black ears, and a clear black face—actually, it's not just black—a clear *bluish*-black face fringed with a full, elegant beard."

"Very good," said the taxidermist. "Much better than what I have. Please continue." He had picked up a pen and was writing down what Henry had said.

"I'd say," continued Henry, "that Virgil's body is robust and well built, served by long, attractive limbs, flexible and strong—they *look* flexible and strong—with a powerful hand or prehensile foot at the end of each. His narrow hands have long digits, as do the feet."

"Oh, yes," the taxidermist interrupted. "Virgil plays the piano. He's a very good player. He can play on his own a Brahms 'Hungarian Dance' for piano four hands. As a final flourish, he curls up his tail and taps the last note with it, bringing down the house. And look at the patterns on his hands and feet."

Henry looked. He went on. "I'd say the palms of his hands and feet are black and covered"—he paused and examined them from different angles to get the play of light—"are black and *filigreed* with loops and whorls that look like the finest silverwork."

"That's absolutely right," said the taxidermist.

"I'd say his long tail, longer than the rest of him, the pride and joy of him, is as dextrous as a hand, with a grip like a constrictor's coil."

"But it also has fine motor control. He plays chess with it. Virgil—"

Henry raised a hand to stop the taxidermist. "A tail with a grip like a constrictor's coil, yet with a deftness of touch that allows him to move a pawn on a chessboard with it."

What other details would Beatrice notice? Henry wondered. He peered into Virgil's mouth.

"And he has good teeth—why does no one ever mention that? Or the detail I notice every day without fail: his lovely dark nails, shiny and slightly bulbous, so that the tip of his every finger and toe glistens like a large dewdrop." Henry was pleased to be speaking in Beatrice's voice.

"Excellent, excellent," muttered the taxidermist. He was writing as fast as he could.

"And I have yet to describe his most eye-catching attribute, that which earns him half his species name: his fur." Henry lightly ran his hand over Virgil's back. "It's soft, thick and lustrous, the back brick-red in colour, while the head and the limbs have more of a chestnut hue. In sunlight, when Virgil is in motion, climbing trees and jumping from one branch to another while I stand, four-footed and rooted to the ground, there is something of molten copper to his movements, a direct, unspoiled ease to even the simplest gesture, dazzling to watch."

"That's Virgil to a letter," exclaimed the taxidermist.

"Good." A conventional descriptive job, matching a concrete reality with its most obvious verbal counterparts, yet Henry too was pleased. It had been such a long time since he had made this kind of effort.

"And his howl?"

The taxidermist returned to the cassette player, rewound the tape and played it a second time. Erasmus immediately started up again in the next room. Henry and the taxidermist ignored him.

"The sound quality isn't very good," Henry said.

"No, it isn't. It was recorded more than forty years ago in the jungles of the upper Amazon."

The howl had that quality, of something coming from far away long ago. It had survived—it was there, coming through all the crackling—but Henry was as much aware of the span of time and gulf of distance over which it had improbably bounded as he was of the howl itself.

"I don't know. It's hard to put into words," he said.

The taxidermist played the howl a third time. Erasmus was properly howling himself in the next room.

Henry shook his head. "Nothing's coming to me at the moment," he said. "Sounds are hard to describe. And my dog is distracting me."

The taxidermist stared at him blankly. Was he disappointed? Piqued?

"I'll have to wait for the muse to whisper to me," Henry said. He felt a weight of weariness descending on him. "I have an idea. I'll think about the howl. In the meantime, in exchange, write something for me about taxidermy. Don't overthink it. Just dash some thoughts onto the page. That's always a good writing exercise."

The taxidermist nodded, but Henry wasn't sure if it was in agreement.

"And why don't you give me your play? I'll read it and tell you what I think."

The taxidermist's reply was short: "I don't want to." Henry heard the definite tone. The full stop in his refusal had resounded like the pad of a judge's gavel being struck. There would be no appeal, or even any explanation, about why he didn't want Henry to read his play.

"But take the cassette player with you. That way you can listen to the howl again while you're working on it."

Henry had not bargained on that.

"I noticed you were looking at the monkey skull mounted on the golden rod," the taxidermist continued.

"Yes, I was. It's striking."

"It's the skull of a howler monkey."

"It is?" Henry felt a quiver of horror.

"Yes."

"But not Virgil's?"

"No. Virgil's skull is inside Virgil's head."

Thirty minutes later Henry walked out of the store, an impatient Erasmus pulling at his leash. It was good to be out in the brisk air again. Henry was late for rehearsal but he entered the small grocery store anyway. He asked if he could have a dish of water for Erasmus. The man behind the counter kindly obliged.

"That's quite the store around the corner," Henry said to him.

"Yeah. It's been there since the dinosaurs went home."

"What's he like, the man who runs it?"

"Crazy old man. Gets into fights with the whole neighbourhood. Comes in here to do two things and only two things: to buy pears and bananas and to make photocopies."

"I guess he likes pears and bananas and he doesn't have a photocopier."

"I guess so. I'm amazed his business survives. Is there really a market for stuffed aardvarks?"

Henry didn't mention the expensive monkey's skull that was in the bag he had gingerly placed on the floor. Skull and glass dome had been packed so that they would arrive safe and sound at their destination. There was also the wolf, the still one, not the leaping one, that had interested Henry, but he had managed to check his impulse.

The man looked at what he had placed on the counter.

"Now there's a vintage piece of technology. Haven't seen a cassette player like that since I was a kid," he said.

"Old and reliable," Henry replied, picking up his precious cargo and heading for the door. "Thank you for the water."

In the taxi home, Erasmus collapsed on the floor and fell asleep right away. Henry thought about the taxidermist. He was not conventionally attractive, fell on the unhandsome side of ordinary, with an inexpressive face that did not project what it was thinking or feeling. Yet those dark staring eyes! His presence had a suffocating quality, but at the same time he radiated a certain magnetism. Or did that appeal come from all the glass-eyed animals surrounding him? Strange that someone so involved with animals should react so little—in fact, not at all—to a live one right in front of him. The taxidermist hadn't even glanced at Erasmus.

Henry thought of him again as a man with a mask. But he'd given the taxidermist a task, to write something about his trade. That should start to make him less of a sphinx. Henry reflected on his day. He had started it meaning only to drop off a card, and now he was loaded down with goods from Okapi Taxidermy and committed to returning.

As soon as he got home, he told Sarah.

"I met the most amazing man," he told her. "This old taxidermist. A shop like you wouldn't believe. All of creation stuffed into one large room. His name's Henry, as it happens. An odd fish. I couldn't place him at all. He's written a play and he wants my help."

"What kind of help?" she asked.

"Help writing it, I think."

"What's it about?"

"I'm not sure. There are two characters, a monkey and a donkey. They're quite focussed on food."

"Is it for children?"

"I don't think so. In fact, it reminded me of . . ." but Henry let his voice trail off. He didn't want to mention what the play reminded him of. "The monkey isn't popular," he said instead.

Sarah nodded her head. "So you've been roped into becoming a collaborator without even knowing what the story's about?"

"I guess so."

"Well, you seem excited. That's nice to see," said Sarah.

She was right. Henry's mind was racing.

The next day Henry went to the main public library to do research on howler monkeys. He discovered odds and ends about the species, that they live in matrilineal groups, for example, and that they keep no fixed territory but over time roam the forest, searching for food and avoiding threats. That evening, after locking Erasmus in the farthest room, he set the cassette player next to the computer and listened to the howl again. He tried to describe it from Beatrice's perspective. If he remembered correctly, she was talking to an imaginary person while she was waiting for Virgil to come back from foraging for food:

BEATRICE: As for the other quality that gives Virgil his name, how to put into words something so astounding to the ears? Words are cold, muddy toads trying to understand sprites dancing in a field—but they're all we have. I will try.

A howl, a roar, a howling roar, a deafening roar— these barely hint at the reality. To compare it to other animals' cries becomes a kind of zoological one-upmanship that addresses only the aspect of volume. A howler monkey's roar exceeds in volume the cry of a peafowl, of a jaguar, of a lion, of a gorilla, of an elephant—at which point the inflating of hulk stops, at least on land. In the ocean, the blue whale, which can weigh well over one hundred and fifty tons, the largest animal ever to grace this planet, can put out a cry at a volume of one hundred and eighty decibels, which is louder than a jet engine, but this cry is at a very low frequency, hardly audible to a donkey, which is probably why we call the whale's cry a *song*. But we must, in all fairness, grant the blue whale top spot. So there, if they were lined up side by side, between the massive bull elephant and the colossal blue whale, involving a serious dropping of the eyes, stands Virgil and his kind, without a doubt the most noise per kilo of any life-form on earth.

One could endlessly dither about the carrying power of a howler's howl. Two miles, three miles, heard over hills, heard against contrary winds— various observers have given their estimates. But the *nature* of Virgil's howl, its aural quality, goes missing in all these measures. I have, on occasion, heard sounds that reminded me of it. Once Virgil and I were walking by a hog farm while a herd was being roughly moved out of an enclosure. Panic set in among the animals and they started up, and that sound, of an entire herd of swine barking and squealing in distress, collectively, brought to my mind something of Virgil's howl.

Another time we encountered a heavily loaded wagon whose axles had not been greased in a long while. Every so often the undercarriage let out a pent-up, bone-crunching squeak, dry and thunderous, which, had it been magnified a hundredfold, would also have conveyed some of the life and power of Virgil's cry.

And I read once a description in Apuleius, my favourite classical writer, of an earthquake that made "a hollow, bellowing noise" and this image, of the earth itself in crisis, moaning and groaning, also clothes well enough in words Virgil's holler.

> But ultimately there is only the thing itself, in its
> raw purity. Hearing is believing.

Henry returned to see the taxidermist within a few days. He was nervous about holding on to his obsolete cassette player and the precious tape, but he was also eager to share with him what he had written.

Henry brought Erasmus again, but this time he tied him outside. The taxidermist seemed neither pleased nor displeased to see him. Henry was confused. He had phoned the taxidermist to tell him he would be coming. They had agreed on a time. Henry wondered if he had made a mistake and if he was late or early. But it just seemed to be the taxidermist's manner, the way he was. He was wearing an apron and was moving a wild boar into the workshop when Henry entered the store.

"Need help?" Henry asked.

The taxidermist shook his head without saying a word. Henry stood and waited, marvelling at the animals. He was happy to be back. This was a room full of adjectives, like a Victorian novel.

"Come in," said the taxidermist from the back room. Henry turned in to it. The taxidermist was already sitting at his desk. Henry sat on the stool again, like an obedient junior clerk. He handed the taxidermist the part he had written for Beatrice. While the other man read, which he did slowly, Henry looked around. The taxidermist had finished the deer he was working on when Henry had first visited. But the other mannequin, the round one, was no further advanced. As for Virgil and Beatrice, they were still in conversation.

"I don't like the jet engine," the taxidermist started, without any preliminaries. "And I'm not sure about the hog farm. But I like the idea of a whole herd of animals. And the dry axle, very good. I can see it. Who's Apuleius? I've never heard of him."

Was it the forgetfulness of old age or personal incapacity that made the man able to say please but not thank you?

"As I say in the text, he's a writer," replied Henry. "His most famous book is *The Golden Ass*, which is why I thought I'd make him Beatrice's favourite classical writer."

He nodded. Henry wasn't sure whether he was assenting to what he, Henry, had just said, or was agreeing with his own private thoughts.

"And you, what do you have? Did you manage to write something on taxidermy?"

The taxidermist nodded and picked up some papers from off his desk. He looked at them for several seconds. Then he just started reading aloud to Henry:

The animal is lost from us, has been taken out of us. I don't just mean in our city lives. I also mean in nature. You go out there, and they're gone, the ordinary and the unusual, they're two-thirds gone. True, in some places you still see them in abundance, but these are sanctuaries and reserves, parks and zoos, special places. The ordinary mixing with animals is gone.

People object to hunting. That is not my problem. Taxidermy does not create a demand; it preserves a result. Were it not for our efforts, animals that have disappeared from the plains of their natural habitat would also disappear from the plains of our imagination. Take the quagga, a subspecies of the common zebra, now extinct. Without the preserved specimens now on display here and there, it would only be a word.

There are five steps in preparing an animal: skinning, curing the hide, preparing the mannequin, fitting the hide onto the mannequin, and finishing. Each step, if well done, is time-consuming. Fruitful patience is what separates the amateur from the professional taxidermist. Much time is spent on the ears, eyes and nose of a mammal so that they are balanced, the eyes not crossed, the nose not bent, the ears not standing unnaturally, the whole giving the animal a coherent expression. The body of the animal is then given a posture that reflects this expression.

We do not use the word *stuffed* anymore since it is simply not true. The animal that meets a taxidermist is no longer stuffed like a bag with moss, spices, tobacco, or whatnot. Science has shed its practical light on us as it has on every discipline. The animal is rather "mounted" or "prepared", and the process is scientific.

Fish are hardly done these days. That part of the

business has died faster than the rest. The camera can preserve the prize catch quicker and cheaper than the taxidermist, and with the owner standing right next to it, for proof. The camera has been very bad for the business of taxidermy. As if the forgotten pages of a photo album were better than a wall holding up the real thing.

We get animals as a result of attrition in zoological gardens. Hunters and trappers are an obvious source of animals; in this case, the supplier is also the customer. Some animals are found dead, killed by disease or as a result of an encounter with a predator. Others are roadkill. The by-products of food-making supply us with the skins and skeletons of swine, cattle, ostriches, and the like, or with stranger fare from more exotic parts of the world— my okapi, for example.

Skinning an animal must be the taxidermist's first perfection. If it is not done well, there will be a price to pay later. It is like the gathering of evidence for the historian. Any flaw at this stage may be impossible to fix later on. If the subcutaneous ends of a bird's tail feathers are cut, for example, they will be much harder to set in a way that looks natural. Mind you, the animal might come to the taxidermist already damaged, whether when it was killed by a hunter or by another animal in a zoo or in a collision with a vehicle. Blood, dirt and other spoilage can be dealt with, and damaged skin or feathers can, within reason, be repaired, but there are limits to what we can do. The evidence can be so ruined as to prevent a proper interpretation of the event, to use the language of the historian.

The mannequin, the form upon which the skin will be placed, must be built. Any number of frames and fillings can be used, and have been used, or better yet, a mannequin can be made from balsa wood. For more elaborate projects, a mannequin is made of clay on a wire armature, a mould is built around it, perhaps in several pieces, and then a cast of fibreglass or polyurethane resin is made, resulting in a mannequin that is light and strong.

Sewing thread must match the colour of the fur. The stitching is done close and tight, with care being taken that the amount of skin taken from each side of the stitch line is the same so that the skin is not stretched unevenly. A figure-eight stitch is used because it brings the edges of the skin together without forming a ridge. Linen thread, which is strong and does not rot, is the best.

The advantage of retaining the skull of an animal in its mounted version is that it can then be displayed open-mouthed, with its real teeth showing. Otherwise, on a mannequin head, the mouth must be sewn shut, or an elaborate mouth must be constructed, with artificial gums, teeth, and tongue. The tongue is the hardest animal part to get right. No matter the effort we put in, it always looks either too dull or too shiny. It's generally not a problem to keep the mouth shut—but what of the snarling tiger or the snapping crocodile, whose mouths are so expressive?

The pose given to the animal, at least the mammal or

the bird, is a crucial matter. Standing straight, skulking, leaping, tense, relaxed, lying on its side, wings out, wings tucked in, and so on—the decision must be made early on since it will affect the making of the mannequin and will play a crucial role in the expressiveness of the animal. The choice is usually between the theatrical or the neutral, between the animal in action or the animal at rest. Each choice conveys a different feel, the first of liveliness captured, the second of waiting. From that, we get two different taxidermic philosophies. In the first, the liveliness of the animal denies death, claims that time has merely stopped. In the second, the fact of death is accepted and the animal is simply waiting for time to end.

The difference is immediately grasped between a stiff, glazed-eyed animal that is standing unnaturally and one that looks moist with life and seemingly ready to jump. Yet that contrast rests on the smallest, most particular details. The key to taxidermic success is subtle, the result obvious.

The layout of animals in a habitat setting or diorama is as carefully thought-out as the blocking of actors on a stage. When done well, when professionals are at work, the effect is powerful, a true glimpse of nature as it was. Look at the crouch of the animal at the river's edge, look at the playfulness of the cubs in the grass, see how that gibbon hangs upside down—it's as if they were alive once again and nothing had happened.

There is no excuse for bad work. To ruin an animal

with shoddy taxidermy is to forfeit the only true canvas we have on which to represent it, and it condemns us to amnesia, ignorance and incomprehension.

There was a time when every good family brightened up its living room with a mounted animal or a case of birds, some representative from the forest that remained in the home while the forest retreated. That business has all dried up, not only the collecting but the preserving. Now the living room is likely to be dull and the forest silent.

Is there a level of barbarism involved in taxidermy? I see none. Or only if one lives a life entirely sheltered from death in which one never looks into the back room of a butcher shop, or the operating room of a hospital, or the working room of a funeral parlour. Life and death live and die in exactly the same spot, the body. It is from there that both babies and cancers are born. To ignore death, then, is to ignore life. I no more mind the smell of an animal's carcass than I do the smell of a field; both are natural and each has its attaching particularity.

And let me repeat: taxidermists do not create a demand. We merely preserve a result. I have never hunted in my life and have no interest in the pursuit. I would never harm an animal. They are my friends. When I work on an animal, I work in the knowledge that nothing I do can alter its life, which is past. What I am actually doing is extracting and refining memory from death. In that, I am no different from a historian, who parses through the material evidence of the past in an attempt to reconstruct it and then understand it. Every animal I have mounted has been an interpretation of the past. I am a historian, dealing with an animal's past; the zookeeper is a politician, dealing with an animal's present; and everyone else is a citizen who must decide on that animal's future. So you see, we are dealing here with matters so much weightier than what to do with a dusty stuffed duck inherited from an uncle.

I should mention a development of the last few years, what has been called art taxidermy. Art taxidermists seek not to imitate nature but to create new, impossible species. They—that is, the artist directing the taxidermist—attach one part of an animal to another part of another, so the head of a sheep to the body of a dog, or the head of a rabbit to the body of a chicken, or the head of a bull to the body of an ostrich, and so on. The combinations are endless, often ghoulish, at times disturbing. I don't know what they mean to do. They are no longer exploring animal nature, that is clear. I think they are rather exploring human nature, often at its most tortured. I cannot say it is to my taste, it certainly goes against my training, but what of that? It continues a dialogue with animals, however odd, and must serve the purpose of some people.

Insects are the eternal enemy of taxidermy and have to be exterminated at every stage. Our other enemies are dust and excessive sunlight. But the worst enemy of taxidermy, and also of animals, is indifference. The indifference of the many, combined with the active hatred of the few, has sealed the fate of animals.

I became a taxidermist because of the writer Gustave Flaubert. It was his story "The Legend of Saint Julian Hospitator" that inspired me. My first animals were a mouse and then a pigeon, the same animals that Julian first kills. I wanted to see if something could be saved once the irreparable had been done. That is why I became a taxidermist: to bear witness.

The taxidermist looked up at Henry from his papers. He said, "Then I have a list and brief descriptions of famous displays in various museums, from single animals to full dioramas."

"Let's leave that for later," Henry said. "I'm thirsty. Could I have some water, please?"

"There are glasses on the edge of the sink."

Henry walked over. He rinsed a glass, filled it, and drank. The skeleton of a rabbit was soaking in a blue chemical solution in a plastic tub at the bottom of the sink. He drank several glassfuls of water. It was very dry in the store and his throat was parched. He was hungry too, for that matter.

Henry thought about what the taxidermist had just read to him. To read on one's own and to be read to are two very different experiences. Not being in control of the words submitted to his attention, unable to establish his own pace but rather dangling along like a prisoner in a chain gang, he found that his level of attention and retention had varied. It had been interesting enough, this discourse on taxidermy, but not highly personal. He still knew nothing about the taxidermist himself.

He remembered the advice of a friend who taught creative writing. "A story begins with three good words," she'd said. "That's where you start when reading a student's submission: find three good words." That wouldn't be hard. At school long ago, the taxidermist had clearly been taught and had learned well the essential elements of prose. And it helped in keeping the listener's attention, at least his, Henry thought, that the subject matter was the odd rather than the mundane, taxidermy rather than fiscal planning.

The glass slipped through Henry's fingers. It shattered on the floor. "I'm sorry. It slipped from my hand."

"Don't worry," responded the taxidermist, unconcerned.

Henry looked around for a broom and a dustpan.

"Leave it, leave it."

Henry's guess was that, being a craftsman, the taxidermist was practical, and small accidents and their clean-ups did not trouble him. Henry walked back to the desk, shards of glass cracking under his shoes. He sat back down on the stool.

"That's good, what you've written," he said to the taxidermist. Now, Henry wondered privately, was the man seeking nothing more than the reassurance of praise, or did he want proper criticism? "Perhaps a little repetitive and disjointed at times, but clear and informative."

The taxidermist said nothing, just looked at Henry, deadpan.

"I noticed how as you went along you started using the personal pronoun 'I' more often. That's good in a first-person narrative. You want to stay rooted in the experience of the individual and not lose yourself in generalities."

Still nothing.

"With that kind of a smooth flow to your writing, your play must be coming along nicely."

"It's not."

"Why's that?"

"I'm stuck. It doesn't work."

The taxidermist admitted to his creative block without any showy frustration.

"Have you finished a first draft?"

"Many times."

"How long have you been working on your play?"

"All my life."

The man rose from his desk and walked to the sink. *Crackle, crackle*, went the glass under his feet. From a shelf under a counter, he produced a brush and a dustpan. He swept the floor clean. Then he picked up some rubber gloves and put them on. He bent over the sink. The silence did not weigh on him. Henry observed him and after a moment saw him in a different light. He was an old man. An old man stooped over a sink, working. Did he have a wife, children? His fingers were bare of rings, but that could be because of the nature of his work. A widower? Henry looked at the man's face in profile. What was beyond that blankness? Loneliness? Worry? Frustrated ambition?

The taxidermist straightened himself. The rabbit skeleton was in his giant hands. It was in one piece, each bone still connected to the next. It was very white and looked small and fragile. He turned it over, inspecting it cautiously. He might have been handling a tiny baby.

A one-story man, a di Lampedusa struggling with his *Leopard*, thought Henry. Creative block is no laughing matter, or only to those sodden spirits who've never even tried to make their personal mark. It's not just a particular endeavour, a job, that is negated, it's your whole being. It's the dying of a small god within you, a part you thought might have immortality. When you're creatively blocked, you're left with—Henry looked around the workshop—you're left with dead skins.

The taxidermist turned the tap on and rinsed the skeleton in a gentle stream of water. He shook the rabbit again and then placed it on the counter next to the sink.

"Why a monkey and a donkey? You told me how you got these two here." Henry reached out and touched the donkey. He was surprised at how springy and woolly its coat was. "But why these particular animals for your story?"

"Because monkeys are thought to be clever and nimble, and donkeys are thought to be stubborn and hardworking. Those are the characteristics that animals need to survive. It makes them flexible and resourceful, able to adapt to changing conditions."

"I see. Tell me more about your play. What happens after the scene with the pear?"

"I'll read it to you."

He removed his gloves, wiped his hands on the apron around his waist, and returned to his desk. He fished through papers.

"Here it is," he said. The taxidermist read aloud again, stage directions and everything:

BEATRICE: (*sadly*) I wish you had a pear.
VIRGIL: And if I had one, I would give it to you.
(*Silence.*)

"That's the end of the opening scene," he said. "Beatrice hasn't ever eaten a pear in her life, or even seen one, and Virgil tries to describe one for her."

"Yes, I remember."

He continued:

BEATRICE: What a pleasant day.
VIRGIL: So warm.
BEATRICE: And sunny.
(*Pause.*)
BEATRICE: What should we do?
VIRGIL: Is there anything we can do?
BEATRICE: (*looking up the road*) We could move on.
VIRGIL: We've done that before and it didn't get us anywhere.
BEATRICE: Maybe this time it will.
VIRGIL: Maybe.

(*They do not move.*)

VIRGIL: We could just talk.

BEATRICE: Talk won't save us.

VIRGIL: But it's better than silence.

(*Silence.*)

BEATRICE: It is.

VIRGIL: I was thinking about faith.

BEATRICE: Were you?

VIRGIL: To my mind, faith is like being in the sun. When you are in the sun, can you avoid creating a shadow? Can you shake that area of darkness that clings to you, always shaped like you, as if constantly to remind you of yourself? You can't. This shadow is doubt. And it goes wherever you go as long as you stay in the sun. And who wouldn't want to be in the sun?

BEATRICE: But the sun has gone, Virgil, gone! (*She bursts into tears and begins to sob loudly.*)

VIRGIL: (*stroking her shoulder to comfort her*) Beatrice, Beatrice. (*But Virgil in turn loses his composure and begins to weep uncontrollably. The two animals bawl for several minutes.*)

He stopped. That even, expressionless style he had of reading was really quite effective, Henry decided. He brought his hands up and quietly made the motion of clapping.

"That's excellent," he said. "I like that analogy between the sun and faith."

The taxidermist nodded slightly.

"And when Virgil says that talk is better than silence, and there's a long silence that follows, broken by Beatrice saying, 'It is,' I can see that working well onstage."

Again, no definite reaction. I should get used to it, Henry told himself. It was likely shyness.

"This sudden darkness—with Beatrice bursting into tears—that's also a nice contrast in tone with the lighter first scene. By the way, where is the play set? I didn't get that."

"It was on the first page."

"Yes, I know, they're in some park or forest."

"No, before that."

"There wasn't anything before that."

"I thought I had copied it," said the taxidermist.

He gave Henry three pages. The first page contained the following information:

A 20th-Century Shirt
_____

A Play in Two Acts

The second page:

Virgil, a red howler monkey
Beatrice, a donkey
A boy and his two friends

And the third page:

```
A country road. A tree.
Late afternoon.

The province of Lower Back,
in a country called the Shirt,
a country like any other,
neighbour to, bigger than,
smaller than, Hat, Gloves,
Jacket, Coat, Trousers,
Socks, Boots and so on.
```

"The story is set on a shirt?" Henry asked, puzzled.

"Yes, on the back of it."

"Well, either Beatrice and Virgil are smaller than bread crumbs or it's a very big shirt."

"It's a very big shirt."

"On which two animals are moving about? And there's a tree and a country road?"

"And more. It's symbolic."

Henry wished he had said that first. "Yes, clearly it's symbolic. But symbolic of *what*? The reader must recognize what the symbol stands for."

"The United States of America, the United Clothes of Europe, the Union of African Shoes, the Association of Asian Hats—names are arbitrary. We parcel out the Earth, give names to landscapes, draw maps, and then we make ourselves at home."

"Is this a play for children? Have I read it wrong?"

"No, not at all. Is your story for children?"

The taxidermist was looking at Henry directly, but he always did. Henry couldn't detect any irony in his voice.

"No, it's not for children. I wrote my novels for adults," he replied.

"The same with my play."

"It's for adults despite the characters and the setting."

"It's for adults *because* of the characters and the setting."

"Point taken. But again, why a shirt? What's the symbolism there?"

"Shirts are found in every country, among every people."

"It's the universal resonance of it?"

"Yes. Every day we put on shirts."

"We all live on the Shirt, is that what you're saying?"

"That's right. Coat, Shirt, Trousers, but it could have been Germany, Poland, Hungary."

"I see." Henry thought for a moment. "Why did you choose those three countries?" he asked.

"What—Coat, Shirt, Trousers?"

"No. Germany, Poland, Hungary."

"They were the first three countries to pop into my head," the taxidermist replied.

Henry nodded. "So the Shirt—it's just the name of the country?"

The taxidermist leaned forward and took his papers

back. "That's what it says here," he said. "'A country like any other, neighbour to, bigger than, smaller than.'"

Henry decided to try constructive criticism. "I'm wondering if maybe something isn't being lost here. One of the important concerns when telling a story is making sure that what is in your head finds its way onto the page. If you want your reader to see what you're seeing, you have to—"

"It's a striped shirt," the taxidermist said, cleanly interrupting Henry.

"Striped?"

"Yes. Vertical stripes. The sun is setting." He searched through his papers. "They've been talking about God and Virgil's faith and the day of the week. They're not sure what day it is. I'll read that scene. Found it."

He started off once again:

BEATRICE: Fine. Have your godless days. Why don't we say Mondays, Tuesdays and Wednesdays? Hesitate on Thursdays, and then embrace on Fridays, Saturdays and Sundays. Does that sound good?

VIRGIL: But there's evil every day of the week.

BEATRICE: Because we're around every day of the week.

VIRGIL: We've done nothing wrong! But speaking of which, what day is it today?

BEATRICE: Saturday.

VIRGIL: I thought it was Friday.

BEATRICE: Maybe it's Sunday.

VIRGIL: I think it's Tuesday.

BEATRICE: Is it possibly Monday?

  VIRGIL: Perhaps it's Wednesday.

BEATRICE: It must be Thursday then.

  VIRGIL: God help us.

           (*Pause.*)

  VIRGIL: I can't take much more of this.

BEATRICE: Then stop thinking. Or think in right measure, as
           far as you can usefully. Then break into prayer. And
           after you've prayed, get back to the building work of
           goodness. There's good every day of the week too.

  VIRGIL: I can't pray. It must be Tuesday, one of my godless
           days.

BEATRICE: Then let's talk about God again on Friday. Until
           then, think of this: perhaps God is silent so that He
           might hear us better.

           (*Silence.*)

  VIRGIL: (*sniffing the air distractedly*) How is it that you know
           so much about bananas? I should be the expert on
           bananas. (*He sniffs the air again.*)

He looked up. "In the opening scene, in describing the
pear, they also talk about bananas. Beatrice knows a lot
about bananas. But the important thing here is that Virgil is
sniffing the air."

Henry nodded. The taxidermist continued:

  VIRGIL: . . . I should be the expert on bananas. (*He sniffs the
           air again.*)

BEATRICE: I like bananas too. Bananas are good.

VIRGIL: As good as coffee.

BEATRICE: As good as cake.

"They're starving," he explained.

VIRGIL: (*sniffing the air more urgently, then in a whisper*) The wind.

BEATRICE: (*nodding her head in agreement, inhaling deeply*) And what a lovely view.

(*The animals stand, Virgil leaning against Beatrice, their nostrils flared, their ears twitching, their eyes wide open.*

Daylight has reached its last hour. The earth and the trunks of the trees are burnished red by the setting sun. Sweeping through the land comes a wind, a most gentle of cavalry charges. It's a fragrant wind, smelling of soil and root, of flower and haystack, of field and forest, of smoke and animals, but also carrying, by virtue of the distances it has covered, the very smell of vastness, a smell moist and cavernous. It's a beautiful wind, an exciting wind, a giving wind. Riding upon it is the collective news of all nature.

In a province dismissed as flat and featureless, upon a clear and cloudless sundown, the Shirt, by means of a simple road, has tricked the two animals into climbing atop a low hill and then has dropped the blindfold before their eyes so that they might see what is to be seen, a landscape that opens up like a philanthropist's wallet.

It starts with a clearing of untended grass, on whose edge, next to the road, the animals are standing. The shrubs and trees nearby are shapely, with full heads of shimmering leaves, and their long shadows are printed onto the land by the orange sun. Next to the clearing is a bright green pasture. Beyond it lies a tilled field of rich brown earth whose furrows make it look like fat corduroy fabric. And there are more fields beyond, a sweep of swells and undulations that stretches out as far as the eye can see. A few hills sprout sprigs of forest, some fields lie green for sheep and cattle, others lie fallow, but most are cultivated, revealing soil of such glossy, mineral wealth that the land sparkles in the sun like an ocean. These endless furrows are waves, and teeming in them is the plankton of the land—bacteria, fungi, mites, all manner of worms and insects—and speeding and jumping about them are the fish of the earth, the mice, moles, voles, shrews, rabbits and others, ever on the lookout for sharkish foxes. Birds chirp and screech as excitedly as gulls above the seas, beside themselves with the living riches over which they hover and to which they have access with an easy buckling of the wings. And access these riches they do. Virgil and Beatrice see countless birds soaring and plummeting and rising up again, their wings beating, the life in the soil scrambling, and all of it—all of it—doused with sprays of wind.

Before long, the light grows dimmer, the hues deeper, and darkness begins to fall upon the land. While the wind

continues to conduct its usual barter, one spore for one
smell, the Shirt now appears marked with immense blue
and grey stripes that traverse it from north to south.)

The taxidermist lifted his eyes and spoke. "I imagine these stripes being projected not only on the back wall but right across the stage and onto the spectators. The whole theatre will be printed in blue and grey stripes."

"What about the landscape?"

"It will also be projected onto the wall, like the posters about Virgil. The stage will be bare, except for the tree to the side. The most prominent feature will be the huge back wall, probably curved, like the wall for a diorama."

"And the wind?"

"Loudspeakers. They do amazing things nowadays with sound systems. The description I give of the wind is just to give the sound designer an idea. I imagine Virgil and Beatrice standing motionless and this wind being heard very distinctly for a good minute or two, a soft, rich wind. Then the landscape will be projected and after that the stripes."

He returned to his text:

VIRGIL: Can you see the stripes? (*pointing at the blue stripes in the failing light*) There and there.

BEATRICE: I've never seen them before.

VIRGIL: Nor have I.

BEATRICE: I imagined one had to be on a mountaintop in Collar to see them.

"Collar is another province," the taxidermist informed Henry.

"Yes, I understood that."

VIRGIL: Clouds and mist must get in the way.

BEATRICE: I'm not sure I believed they actually existed.

VIRGIL: The stripes are glowing.

BEATRICE: As bright as an aquarium at night.

VIRGIL: As bright as the truth.

(*Pause.*)

VIRGIL: (*crestfallen, placing his hands on the sides of his face*) How can there be anything beautiful after what we've lived through? It's incomprehensible. It's an insult. (*He stamps the ground with a foot.*) Oh, Beatrice, how are we going to talk about what happened to us one day when it's over?

(*Pause.*)

BEATRICE: I don't know.

(*Letting go of Beatrice's leg and falling onto all fours, Virgil begins to howl. The landscape and stage slowly fade to darkness to the sound of Virgil loudly expressing his outrage.*)

"And then we'd hear Virgil's howl, starting with his alone, then augmented by other howler monkeys' howls and projected through the sound system. I want a great and terrible symphony of howls."

"Why does the Shirt have stripes? Why that detail? It reminds me of—"

The doorbell tinkled. Without a word or gesture to Henry, the taxidermist stood up and left for the showroom. Henry sighed and looked at Virgil and Beatrice.

"Does he always interrupt you like this?" he asked Virgil.

Henry remembered the bell in the Flaubert story, when the stag comes up to Julian, just before it curses him. Except that bell must have tolled rather than tinkled. Henry got up and went to look at the newly finished deer head. He could hear the taxidermist speaking to someone in the other room. Henry drank more water at the sink, holding a new glass with both hands. He examined the rabbit. It still had its ligaments, which is why the skeleton hadn't fallen to pieces. The ligaments looked like thin spaghetti.

The taxidermist returned. He removed his apron. "I must go," he said curtly.

"That's fine. I should be going, too."

Henry gathered his coat.

"When will you come back?" the taxidermist asked.

He's so damn up-front and direct, with questions that are orders, Henry thought.

"Why don't we go to the zoo together? We have our choice." The city enjoyed the luxury of having two zoos and Henry liked zoos. It was where he'd started his career, in a way. "I'm sure you'd have a fascinating take on live animals. I spent weeks researching—"

"Zoos are bastard patches of wilderness," the taxidermist cut in as he put on his coat. "The animals there are degenerate. They shame me."

Henry was taken aback. "Well, zoos are a compromise, that's for certain, but so is nature. And if it weren't for zoos, most people would never see real—"

"I go only when I have to, for work, to see a live specimen."

Henry could hear in the taxidermist's voice the judge's gavel coming down again. The taxidermist was directing him out of the workshop with broad, imperative gestures.

I *will* get him to bend, thought Henry.

"I see zoos as embassies from the wild, each animal representing its species. In any case, let's meet at the café up the street. The weather is so nice now. How about this coming Sunday at two o'clock? That's what I have time for." Henry put a firm edge to his last words.

"All right. Sunday at two at the café," the taxidermist agreed tonelessly.

Henry was relieved. "I have a question," he followed up smoothly as they passed through the showroom. "It's been on my mind since I read the opening scene from your play: why this minute description of a common fruit? It seems an odd start."

"How did you put it?" replied the taxidermist. "'Words are cold, muddy toads trying to understand spirits dancing in a field'?"

"Yes. I said 'sprites'."

"'But they're all we have.'"

"'But they're all we have,'" Henry repeated.

"Please," the taxidermist said, opening the front door of the store and ushering Henry out. "Reality escapes us. It's beyond description, even a simple pear. Time eats everything."

And with that, leaving Henry with the image of Time eating a pear into oblivion, the taxidermist practically slammed the door in Henry's face. He locked it, turned the cardboard sign hanging from its frame from OPEN to CLOSED, and disappeared back into his workshop. Henry took no offence at the lack of ceremony bordering on rudeness. He must behave like this with everyone, he guessed. It was nothing personal.

At least Erasmus was glad to see him. The dog was jumping up and down, yelping with joy.

Henry had meant to ask the taxidermist another question. On the Shirt, there wasn't only a monkey and a donkey and a tree and a country road and a picturesque landscape. There was also "a boy and his two friends". So there were people in the play too?

At home, Henry told Sarah about his second visit with the taxidermist.

"He's a real character. As surly as a badger. And his play, I can't figure it out. There are animal characters—a monkey and a donkey—and they live on this very large shirt. It's all quite fanciful, yet there are elements that remind me, well, that remind me of the Holocaust."

"The Holocaust? You see the Holocaust in everything."

"I knew you'd say that. Except in this case there's an emphatic reference to striped shirts, for example."

"So?"

"Well, during the Holocaust—"

"Yes, I know about striped shirts and the Holocaust. But Wall Street capitalists also wear striped shirts, for example, as do clowns. Everyone has a striped shirt in their closet."

"Perhaps you're right," Henry said.

He was irked. Sarah had long ago lost interest in the Holocaust, or at least in his creative involvement with it. And she was wrong. It wasn't that he saw the Holocaust in everything. It's that he saw everything in the Holocaust, not only camp victims, but also capitalists and many others, perhaps even clowns.

That Saturday, Henry and Sarah went shopping for the soon-to-come baby. Stroller, bassinet, a sling, the tiniest clothes—they bought these items with a smile stuck on their faces the whole time.

They weren't very far from the taxidermist's store. On an impulse Henry suggested that they drop by. Sarah agreed. It was a mistake. The visit went badly. Standing outside the store, Sarah granted that the okapi looked attractive. But as soon as they entered, Henry could tell Sarah didn't like the place. When the taxidermist emerged from his lair, she seemed to cower. Henry showed her around, pointing out details, trying to elicit an enthusiastic response. Sarah's remarks were short and she mechanically nodded her head in agreement to whatever Henry said. She looked tense. The taxidermist, for his part, glowered. Henry did all the talking.

They'd hardly got home before they started at each other.

"He's helping me," Henry said.

"What do you mean he's *helping* you? How? With that hideous monkey skull he tricked you into buying? What is that monstrosity? Yorick to your Hamlet?"

"I'm getting ideas off him."

"Of course, I'd forgotten. The monkey and the donkey. Winnie the Pooh meets the Holocaust."

"It's not like that."

"THE GUY'S A CREEP! DID YOU SEE THE WAY HE WAS LOOKING AT ME?"

"Why are you shouting at me? People always look at pregnant women. And what does it matter to you who I hang out with? I like his store. It—"

"IT'S A FUCKING FUNERAL PARLOUR! YOU'RE SPENDING YOUR TIME WITH DEAD STUFFED ANIMALS AND A SLEAZY OLD MAN!"

"Would you rather I spend my time in a bar?"

"THAT'S NOT THE POINT!"

"Will you stop shouting at me?"

"IT'S THE ONLY WAY YOU'LL LISTEN!"

And so it went, a full-blown row while bags full of baby things lay around them.

. . .

The next morning, Henry left early for his music lesson. Events conspired to improve his mood. First, his clarinet teacher surprised him with a gift.

"I can't accept this," Henry said.

"What are you talking about? It's from a good friend, an old student. He hasn't used it for a century. He wanted to get rid of it. I got it for practically nothing. What's the point of the thing never being used?"

"I'd like to pay you for it."

"Never! Over my dead body. You'll pay me by playing it beautifully."

Henry was holding in his hands the loveliest Albert system clarinet.

"And I think you're ready to try some Brandwein," his teacher added. "We'll start today."

Maybe my heavy black ox is starting to take off, Henry thought. He was playing all the time, after all. Two tricks helped him. The first was to devote a corner of his apartment exclusively to music playing, with the stand set up, the sheet music in order, the clarinet clean, and a cup in place in which to soak his reeds in warm water. The second was to practice often, but only in short bursts, no more than fifteen minutes. He usually practiced just before a commitment he couldn't miss. That way, if he played well, he stopped regretfully and eager to come back to it, and if he played poorly, he was forced to give up before dejection and exasperation had him wanting to throw the clarinet out the window. With this arrangement, he was practicing three, four times a day.

He had two faithful spectators: Mendelssohn, who was patiently fascinated in the way only cats can be, and the monkey skull, which he had set on the chimney mantel nearby. Their round eyes, the cat's and the skull's, were always on him when he played. Erasmus, the Philistine, would whine and howl, so Henry had to lock him in another room, usually with Sarah.

The weather also soothed Henry. It was a Sunday that was gloriously living up to its pagan name, a bold rebel burst of warm weather that announced the impending vanquishing of winter. Music was escaping from doors and windows that at long last could be left open, and everyone in the city was parading in the streets. Henry arrived early at the café to have a light lunch before his appointment with the taxidermist. A smart thing too, as the place was packed. He got a table right next to the wall, one chair in the sun, one in the shade. He had Erasmus as usual, but he didn't have his normal zip. The dog lay quietly in the shade of the table.

The taxidermist arrived exactly at two, as punctual as a soldier.

"Sunlight, warm wonderful sunlight!" Henry said expansively, his arms open wide.

"Yes," was the taxidermist's full reply.

"Which seat would you like?" Henry asked, rising a little to indicate that he was willing to move.

The taxidermist took the free seat, the one in the shade, without saying a word. Henry settled back. Outside of the confines of his store, the taxidermist looked out of place. He was overdressed considering the warm weather. When the waiter came over, Henry noticed that he addressed the question "What can I get you?" only to him and not to the taxidermist. And the taxidermist wasn't looking at the waiter, either. Henry ordered a latte with a poppy seed pastry.

"And you?" Henry asked.

"I'll have a black coffee," the taxidermist said, staring at the tabletop.

The waiter left without saying a word.

Whether it had started with him not liking them or them not liking him, it was clear that by now the dislike was mutual. It was not hard to imagine that if there was a street association, the fancy bridal store owner, the natty jeweller, the sophisticated restaurateur, the hip café owner and the others would stand on one side of issues, while the old taxidermist, the man who had trucks bringing him the carcasses of dead animals, the man who never smiled or laughed, would stand on the other side. Henry didn't know what the issues were, but there would be issues, that was for sure. Sundays, rainy days, every day, politics gets into everything.

"How are you?"

"Fine."

Henry took a breath and put a firm lid on his high spirits. He would get only monosyllables out of the man if he didn't play it his way. One thing was certain: he wasn't going to mention the previous day's awkward visit with his wife.

"I was thinking," said Henry. "You describe Virgil in your play. You also need to describe Beatrice."

"I do."

"I was thinking that because I saw a donkey a few days ago."

"Where did you see a donkey?"

"At the zoo. I went on my own."

The taxidermist nodded, though without much interest.

"I thought of you when I saw it," Henry continued. "I had a good look at it. You know what I noticed?"

"What?" From the inside breast pocket of his coat, the taxidermist pulled out a pen and a notepad.

"I noticed that a donkey has an appealing terrestrial solidity—it's a good, solid animal—yet its limbs are surprisingly slim. It's as firmly yet lithely connected to the earth as a birch tree. And such lovely, round, compact hooves. And the legs tuck directly under the animal when it's standing still. When it's walking, the stride is dainty and short-stepped. The proportions of the head—the slim ears, the dark eyes, the nose, the mouth, the length of the snout—are very satisfying. The lips are strong and agile. The crunching and grinding sound a donkey makes when it's eating is very soothing to listen to. And its braying is as frank and tragic as a sob."

"That's all very true," the taxidermist said, jotting things down in his notepad.

"Some have a cross in their hair along the back and across the shoulders, exactly like a Christian cross."

"Yes. Coincidence." The taxidermist did not write that detail down.

"So what do they do, Beatrice and Virgil?"

"What do you mean?"

"What do they do in the play? What happens?"

"They talk."

"About what?"

"About many things. I have a scene with me right here. It takes place after they've gone off to look for food and each is afraid of having lost the other. Just after Beatrice goes off to find Virgil, Virgil comes back."

He looked around warily at the other tables. No one was paying them any attention. The taxidermist pulled out of his breast pocket some folded sheets. Henry thought he was finally going to have something to read. Instead, the taxidermist unfolded them in front of his face, leaned forward in his seat and cleared his throat. Even here, in public, he was going to read aloud. What a control freak, Henry thought, exasperated. The taxidermist started in a low voice:

> (*Virgil picks at the ground in front of him, searching for an imaginary tick.*)
>
> BEATRICE: (*appearing from the right*) There you are! I was looking for you.

VIRGIL: I missed you!

BEATRICE: So did I!

(*They embrace.*)

VIRGIL: I was afraid something had happened to you.

BEATRICE: So was I.

VIRGIL: If anything happens to you, I want the same to happen to me.

BEATRICE: I feel the same.

(*Pause.*)

BEATRICE: How's your back?

"Virgil always has a sore back. And Beatrice always has a sore neck," the taxidermist informed Henry. "It's the stress. And she has a limp. The limp is explained later."

BEATRICE: How's your back?

VIRGIL: It's fine. How's your neck?

BEATRICE: Without knots.

VIRGIL: How's your foot?

BEATRICE: Ready for another day.

VIRGIL: I didn't find any food.

BEATRICE: Nor did I.

(*Pause.*)

BEATRICE: What should we do?

VIRGIL: I don't know.

BEATRICE: This road must lead somewhere.

VIRGIL: Is it somewhere we want to be?

BEATRICE: It could be good news.

VIRGIL: It could be bad news.

BEATRICE: Who's to know?

VIRGIL: This is a safe and pleasant spot.

BEATRICE: Danger could be creeping up.

VIRGIL: We should go then?

BEATRICE: We should.

(*They do not move.*)

VIRGIL: I have three jokes.

BEATRICE: This is no time for jokes.

VIRGIL: They're good, I promise.

BEATRICE: I can't anymore. Not laugh, or even try to laugh. About anything.

VIRGIL: Then those criminals have truly robbed us of everything.

The waiter approached their table. The taxidermist stopped reading and held his papers under the table. The waiter placed their coffees and Henry's pastry on the table.

"There you go," said the waiter.

"Thank you."

Henry realized that he had forgotten to ask for two forks. He took the single fork that the waiter had brought and cut the pastry into several pieces. He placed the fork on the taxidermist's side of the plate. He would use his coffee spoon instead.

"Help yourself," Henry said.

The taxidermist shook his head. He brought the play back above the table.

"'Those criminals . . .'" Henry repeated.

The taxidermist nodded and continued:

VIRGIL: Then those criminals have truly robbed us of
          everything.
          (*Pause.*)
BEATRICE: All right, go ahead, tell me your jokes.
VIRGIL: Pity there's no coffee.
BEATRICE: Pity there's no cake.
          (*They settle by the tree again.*)

Henry was struck by the irony of the timing. Just as coffee and cake were delivered to them, Virgil and Beatrice
mourn their absence. And earlier Beatrice had said how the
sun had gone, leaving them without faith, and here they
were basking in the sun. It also struck him how naked and
alive Virgil and Beatrice were, so much more revealing of
themselves than their author.

VIRGIL: Joke Number One. (*He leans over and cups his
          hands around Beatrice's ear. He whispers hotly. Only
          a few words of the joke can be intermittently
          distinguished.*) . . . and a baker . . . the daughter
          says . . . the next day . . . for a whole month . . . he's
          a wreck . . . and then she says . . . (*He delivers the
          punch line.*)
BEATRICE: (*dully, without laughing*) That's funny.
VIRGIL: Joke Number Two. (*Again he whispers into Beatrice's*

> *ear.*) . . . comes up to another prisoner . . . the letter
> U . . . says, pointing to his chest . . . (*Punch line.*)
> BEATRICE: I don't get it.
>   VIRGIL: In Hungarian . . . (*He whispers explanation into her
> ear.*)
> BEATRICE: (*dully, without laughing*) Oh, I see.
>   VIRGIL: Joke Number Three. (*He whispers into her ear.*)
> BEATRICE: (*dully, without laughing*) I've heard that one before.

"They have conversations like that at first," the taxidermist said. "A mixture of passing the time and figuring out what they should do next."

"I like the jokes being whispered. That's good."

"They also speak on their own at times. Soliloquies. Beatrice can still manage restful sleep, even whole nights, and with dreams too. Virgil, however, is a poor sleeper. He always has the same dream: a noise—a boring—that slowly gets louder until he wakes up with a gasp, his eyes popping open like burst balloons, as he puts it. He jokes that he's always dreaming about termites. It's the anxiety."

"Why is Virgil so anxious?"

"Because he's a howler monkey in a world that doesn't want howler monkeys."

Henry nodded.

The taxidermist continued. "When Beatrice is sleeping, Virgil sometimes talks to himself. In the middle of their first night next to the tree, he wakes up and talks about a book called *Jacques the Fatalist and His Master.*"

"Yes, by Denis Diderot," Henry said. A French classic from the eighteenth century. He'd read it long ago.

"I didn't understand it at all," the taxidermist said.

Henry tried to remember the novel. Jacques and his master travel around on their horses, talking about this, that and the other. They tell stories, but are constantly interrupted by events. Jacques is presumably a fatalist and his master is not, though Henry couldn't vouch for it from memory, only assumed so from the title. He couldn't recall having especially "understood" the novel. He remembered only the Gallic lightness and the modern, comic feel of it, a bit like Beckett on horseback.

"Why do you make reference in your play to a novel you didn't understand?" Henry asked.

The taxidermist replied, "I'm not bothered by that fact. I use it because there's an element in it I found useful. Jacques and his master have a discussion on the various injuries a body can suffer and the pain that goes with each. Jacques strongly argues that a knee injury is the champion of hideous, unbearable pains. Virgil can't remember if the example Jacques gives is of falling from a horse and hitting one's knee against a sharp rock or of receiving a musket shot in it. Whatever the case, it convinced Virgil when he read the book. But now, during his soliloquy, he mulls over the measuring and comparing of physical pains. He grants that the kind of knee pain described by Jacques would be blinding, but it would also be a jolt, short and powerful at the moment of impact, but then greatly reduced. How does that compare with the grinding, hindering pain of a bad back? A knee is small, locally linked and comparatively easy not to use. 'To put one's feet up and relax'—the pleasure of not using one's knees is even celebrated in a cliché. But the back is a real railway hub, connected to everything, demands constantly made upon it. And what about the pain of thirst and hunger? Or that entirely different kind of pain, the one that injures no particular organ yet kills the spirit that links them? At this point, Virgil starts to weep but he stops himself so that he doesn't wake Beatrice. This is one soliloquy he has during the play."

"I see."

"He has another one that morning, while Beatrice is still sleeping. Virgil remembers how their miseries started. Started in his mind, that is, the moment when he realized what was happening to them. He acts it out. He's reading his morning paper at his favourite café and his eyes are drawn to one of the headlines. The headline announces a government edict concerning new categories of citizens—or rather, as the article makes clear, a category of citizens and a new category of *non*-citizens. Virgil reads with increasing astonishment as he realizes that he—he himself personally, in all his specific details, this monkey sitting in a café reading a paper, such an ordinary thing—is the exact and intended target."

Henry took mental note: a government edict excluding Virgil. He didn't want to interrupt the taxidermist, who was becoming quite animated. A customer or two glanced over casually. But it was the waiter returning to their table that had an effect on the taxidermist. He brought his hands into his lap and looked down.

"Do you need any help?" the waiter asked Henry. He corrected himself: "Can I get you anything else?"

"No, I'm fine, thank you. Would you like a refill?"

The taxidermist said nothing, only shook his head slightly. He seemed to be pretending he wasn't there.

"I'll just have the bill, please."

"Yes, of course."

Henry had the sense the waiter was about to talk to the taxidermist, but changed his mind and walked away instead.

The taxidermist was bent on finishing his description of Virgil's café scene. He continued rapidly.

"It's the expulsion from Eden! The Fall! In an instant, the newspaper is transmogrified into a giant finger floating in the air, pointing at him. Virgil is filled with apprehension that other patrons at the café, many of them reading the same newspaper, will notice him. Why, over there and over there, didn't they just glance at him? That's how the events entered his life, he laments, as they had entered the lives of so many others, a vast and varied group that included him and Beatrice and others and others and others: with a single moment of realization. In that moment the world shattered like a pane of glass, so that everything looked exactly as it had earlier, and yet was different, now clear and newly sharp with menace. After that—"

The waiter reappeared with the bill. Remarkably quick of

him, Henry thought. Was he wanting to get rid of us? He paid and they stood up. With the taxidermist being mid-story, there was nothing to do but walk towards his store. Though so close, it felt like a different world. Hardly anyone was walking by and it was much quieter than the more commercial end of the street. Henry was disappointed to see black fabric hanging down each of the bay windows. The effect upon turning the corner, which he was looking forward to, was utterly different. In fact, with no okapi peeking out, there wasn't much of an effect at all. Just a fading jungle mural on a brick wall. The taxidermist noticed him looking at the black fabric.

"I don't want people lingering about when the shop is closed. You never know with people," he said, as he fished for keys in the pocket of his coat. He looked around as he said that, scanning the few people who were passing by—a middle-aged couple, a slouching teenager, a lone man.

"You don't like people, do you?" Henry said, which he meant lightly.

The taxidermist looked at the passersby for another moment, then turned his gaze onto Henry—and it was a pinpoint of concentration wholly focussed on him, animal-like in its intensity, exactly that, animal-like. As the taxidermist bore into him with his steady eyes, a single thought occurred to Henry: *I am people.*

Henry made an attempt at an apology. "What I meant is you're comfortable with animals. You know them. Whereas people, people are strange and unreliable. That's what I meant."

The taxidermist turned and unlocked the door of his store without saying a word. They entered. There in the gloom, hidden and quiet, anxiously awaiting his return, were all his animals. He flicked a few switches and the light seemed to bring them to life. The taxidermist was visibly relieved to be back in his store. He headed for the back room. Henry lingered as Erasmus settled on the floor next to the front counter. The dog seemed out of sorts, Henry noted in passing.

When Henry entered the workshop, the taxidermist was already at his desk. Henry took his usual place on the stool. The taxidermist was not to be put off finishing what he was saying. He said it more freely now.

"After the incident reading the paper in the café, Virgil bemoans how his feelings have shrivelled. He corrects himself: he says that one feeling has expanded—fear—while all the others have shrivelled. Intellectual thrill, aesthetic rejoicing, quiet appreciation, fond recollection, witty banter— these have all been crowded out by fear, leaving him dull-eyed and indifferent most of the time. Were it not for Beatrice being in his life, Virgil says, he would feel nothing at all. Everything, even fear, nearly, would be shrugged off. He would be a wandering corpse, a bundle of mindless functions, like a house without its inhabitants. He says that, and then he remembers the landscape of the previous evening, how moved he was by it. Considering his circumstances, this astounds him, that he was moved by a wind and a few fields. Like taking a moment in a museum on fire to appreciate a fine landscape painting."

Henry wondered if the taxidermist didn't live in his store, not above it or nearby, but actually *in* it. He looked at Virgil and Beatrice, nearly said hello to them. He was starting to know them well.

The taxidermist went on, uninterruptible.

"He's so elated at this unexpected burst of feeling that for nothing, for joy, he gets up and cartwheels himself onto his hands. He examines the landscape upside down. He leans to one side and holds himself up in the air on a single arm, which is easy for him. After a moment, he returns onto all fours and he does the same balancing act with his legs, first standing on both and then getting onto just one. That's a harder trick for a howler monkey. They're not normally bipedal. His two arms shake, his raised leg trembles, his tail jerks about in the air. And that's when Beatrice wakes up and asks him the key question of the play."

He searched on his desk. Henry couldn't see why the taxidermist's pages had to be so scattered. He was forever shuffling through them. Why didn't he have them in order? It was a play, after all, a sequence of scenes that should follow some narrative logic.

"Here, I found it," the taxidermist said. And he read— aloud, of course:

BEATRICE: Virgil, you asked a question yesterday.

VIRGIL: (*who has his back to her, swaying, nearly falling, but still managing to stay balanced on one leg*) Oh, you're awake! Good morning. How did you sleep?

BEATRICE: Very well, thank you. Guess what I dreamed about?

VIRGIL: (*still balancing*) What?

BEATRICE: A pear!

VIRGIL: (*still balancing*) But you've never seen one.

BEATRICE: In my dream I certainly did. It was bigger than a pineapple.

VIRGIL: (*still balancing*) Wouldn't that be good.

BEATRICE: You asked a question yesterday.

VIRGIL: (*still balancing*) Did I? How pointless.

BEATRICE: No, it was a good one. I was thinking about it last night as I was falling asleep.

VIRGIL: (*still balancing*) What question was that?

BEATRICE: You asked, "How are we going to talk about what happened to us one day when it's over?"
(*Virgil falls over.*)

VIRGIL: That's assuming we survive.

"That's the key question in the play, how they are going to talk about what happened to them. They come back to the question again and again."

"And to answer the question I asked you at the café," Henry broke in, "about what happens in the play, in effect what happens is they talk about talk."

"I think of it as talking about memory."

If Henry hadn't seen it earlier, he was starting to see now where the problem lay with the taxidermist's play, why he needed help. There seemed to be essentially no action and no plot in it. Just two characters by a tree talking. It had worked with Beckett and Diderot. Mind you, those two were crafty and they packed a lot of action into the apparent inaction. But inaction wasn't working for the author of *A 20th-Century Shirt*.

Henry wanted the taxidermist to explain his play, but he didn't want to be the first to invoke the Holocaust. He thought the taxidermist would be more forthcoming if he brought it up himself.

"Let me ask you a simple question: what's your play about?"

As soon as the question had left Henry's lips, the irony of it leapt to his mind. It was the same question the historian had asked him during that terrible lunch in London nearly three years ago, the question that had gutted and silenced him. And here he was asking it himself. But the taxidermist had no problem dealing with it. He practically shouted his answer.

"It's about them!" His hand violently swept the room.

"Them?"

"The animals! They're two-thirds dead. Do you not understand that?"

"But—"

"In quantity and in variety, put together, two thirds of all animals have been exterminated, wiped out forever. My play is about this"—he searched for words—"this irreparable abomination. Virgil and Beatrice call it—wait!"

The vehemence and conviction of his tone took Henry aback. The taxidermist dove into his papers again. For once he found what he wanted quickly:

BEATRICE: What name will it have?

VIRGIL: That's a good question.

BEATRICE: The Events?

VIRGIL: Not descriptive enough, and it carries no judgment. Name and nature must be combined.

BEATRICE: The Unthinkable? The Unimaginable?

VIRGIL: Why even bother with it if it's unthinkable or unimaginable?

BEATRICE: The Unnameable?

VIRGIL: If we can't even name it, how can we talk about it?

BEATRICE: The Deluge?

VIRGIL: The weather had nothing to do with it.

BEATRICE: The Catastrophe?

VIRGIL: Could be anything, a flood, an earthquake, an explosion in a mine.

BEATRICE: The Searing?

VIRGIL: Could be a forest fire.

BEATRICE: The Terror?

VIRGIL: Sounds like something done quickly, involving running and panting. Not enough calculation to it. Besides, it's been used before.

BEATRICE: The Tohu-bohu?

VIRGIL: Sounds like a dairy-free dessert.

BEATRICE: The Horror?

VIRGIL: That's stronger.

BEATRICE: Even better: the Horror*s*, plural but used in a
singular construction, the curve of the *s* like a ladle
in a soup from hell, serving up the unthinkable and
the unimaginable, the catastrophic and the searing,
the terror and the tohu-bohu.

VIRGIL: We'll call it the Horrors.

BEATRICE: Good.

(*Pause.*)

BEATRICE: So, how are we going to talk about the Horrors?

"You see, the question comes back again and again. Virgil
and Beatrice set up a list, a very important list. Here, look."

The taxidermist abruptly got up from behind his desk.
Henry stood up with him. The taxidermist came round to
Beatrice. Placing one hand on Virgil's rump and the other
under his bent leg, he lifted Virgil off Beatrice's back. He
placed him on the desk.

"Look," he said again.

He was pointing at Beatrice's back. Henry looked. All he
could see was thick donkey hair, a little matted here and
there. The taxidermist went to get his light. When he
shone it on her back, Henry could see a vague pattern in the
way the hair was matted.

"It's the list," the taxidermist said. "Because they live in a country called the Shirt, they call it their sewing kit. Virgil starts writing on Beatrice's back with a wet fingertip a list of all the ways they come up with of how to talk about the Horrors."

Henry looked closely at Beatrice's coat. There was no way that spit and hair could spell anything on a donkey's back, he thought, certainly nothing that would survive the course of an ordinary day, but it was no doubt another of the taxidermist's symbols.

"The first item in the sewing kit is a howl. Beatrice gets the idea from hearing Virgil the previous night. The second item is a black cat."

"A black cat? How is a black cat a way of talking about the Terrors?"

"The Horrors. Like this."

The taxidermist carefully resettled Virgil on top of Beatrice and went back to his papers. Henry mused that it would be so much easier if he could get the play into his own hands and read it. He realized that he was close to thinking *"and write it."*

The taxidermist found a page and read from it:

VIRGIL: To talk-about so that we might live-with—I presume that's why we want to do this?

BEATRICE: Yes. To remember and yet to go on living.

VIRGIL: To know and yet to be happy—or at least content, productive.

BEATRICE: Yes.

VIRGIL: Like living with a cat. Always there, but without taking over our lives. Needs to be fed, needs to be brushed, sometimes needs our full attention, but mostly content to be on its own, lying in a corner, in our presence but not constantly on our mind.

BEATRICE: The Horrors as a howl and as a black cat.

VIRGIL: I must write this down. (*He looks around. He notices Beatrice's back.*) I know where. (*He wets a fingertip with his tongue and writes on Beatrice's coat, laying flat the hairs. He wets his fingertip a number of times. He finishes and looks over his work, satisfied.*) There. We'll call it a sewing kit.

BEATRICE: Sewing kit, knowing kit.

VIRGIL: That's right.

"It's symbolic again," the taxidermist said.

"Yes, I understand that. But all this talking. In a play, as in any story, there must be—"

"There's silence too. At one point Virgil says that words are just 'refined grunts.' 'We overvalue words,' he says. After that, they try to talk about the Horrors by other means, through gestures and sounds and facial expressions. But it exhausts them. The scene is right here in front of my eyes."

He launched forth:

BEATRICE: I'm exhausted. I can't do it anymore.

VIRGIL: Nor can I. Shall we just listen?

BEATRICE: To what?

VIRGIL: To silence, to hear what it has to say.

BEATRICE: All right.

(*Silence.*)

VIRGIL: Hear anything?

BEATRICE: Yes.

VIRGIL: What?

BEATRICE: Silence.

VIRGIL: And what did silence say?

BEATRICE: Nothing.

VIRGIL: You did well. I kept hearing my inner voice saying, "I am listening to silence, hoping to hear something." And I had other noisy stray thoughts.

BEATRICE: Oh, I heard those as well. In different words, but the same thing.

VIRGIL: We should try true silence, emptying our heads of all inner noise.

BEATRICE: I'm willing to try.

VIRGIL: One, two, three, go.

(*Virgil and Beatrice look straight ahead, innerly silent.*

A bumblebee appears. It flies in a straight line in front of Virgil and Beatrice. They follow its loud droning flight, their heads turning from far left to far right, but they say nothing.

A bird chirps loudly in a tree on the left. Virgil and Beatrice look to the left, but say nothing.

A dog barks in the far distance on the right. Virgil and Beatrice look to the right, but say nothing.

> *A frog croaks on the left. They look to the left, but say nothing.*
>
> *Two squirrels scramble up a tree on the right, one in querulous pursuit of the other. They look to the right, but say nothing.*
>
> *An explosion of bird chatter on the left. They look to the left, but say nothing.*
>
> *The screech from a hawk above. They look up, but say nothing.*
>
> *A single leaf falls. Both animals follow its dancing descent. The leaf hits the ground.)*

VIRGIL: Gosh, what a noisy place this is!

BEATRICE: Very distracting.

VIRGIL: Impossible to hear silence.

BEATRICE: I agree.

(*Silence.*)

VIRGIL: I bet you if I made a lot of noise, you'd hear silence better.

BEATRICE: Do you think?

VIRGIL: Why don't we try. (*Virgil stands up. He takes in a big breath. He says the following at top volume.*)
ALL ABOARD, ALL ABOARD! QUICK, QUICK, QUICK! CHOO-CHOO-CHOO-CHOO, DON'T WANT TO MISS THE TRAIN! CHOO-CHOO-CHOO-CHOO, DON'T FORGET YOUR DRINKS AND SNACKS! DON'T WANT TO GO HUNGRY! KEEP AN EYE ON YOUR LUGGAGE! CHOO-CHOO-CHOO! YOU

THERE, WHERE ARE YOU GOING? GET
INTO YOUR CAR. ALL ABOARD, ALL
ABOARD, I SAY! LAST CALL! CHOO-CHOO-
CHOO-CHOO, THE TRAIN IS ABOUT TO
DEPART, CHOO-CHOO-CHOO-CHOO! A
RIDE TO REMEMBER! CHOO-CHOO-CHOO-
CHOO! PREPARE TO DEPART, PREPARE TO
DEPART. (*to Beatrice*) Well, the silence, did you
hear it?

BEATRICE: Yes.

VIRGIL: And?

BEATRICE: It was thousands of shadows pressing on me.

VIRGIL: What were they saying?

BEATRICE: They were lamenting the passing of their unfinished
lives.

VIRGIL: What words did they use?

BEATRICE: None that I could hear.

VIRGIL: How were these words different from regular
silence?

BEATRICE: Hard to say.

VIRGIL: How can we quote them?

BEATRICE: Difficult to put into words.

VIRGIL: What can we say about what they said?

BEATRICE: My tongue is tied.

VIRGIL: If I were reading it, what would I be reading?

BEATRICE: My pen is dry.

VIRGIL: This isn't working. We need a different approach.
(*Silence.*)

"You see, it's not just words. There's also noise and silence. And there are gestures too. Like this one. Virgil and Beatrice put this one in their sewing kit."

The taxidermist made a gesture with his right hand in front of his chest.

"I've done a drawing for the actor," he added.

He held the page in the air above the desk. It was a drawing in four sections.

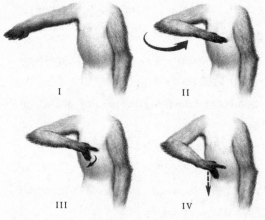

A HORRORS HAND GESTURE

Henry noticed the hairiness of the arms. For this irreparable abomination unto animals, the taxidermist would have the actors dress for the part. The hand was brought in front of the chest, two fingers were pointed down and then the hand dropped down. Why two fingers, he wondered?

"Words, silence, noise, characters, symbols—these are all

important elements in a story," Henry started. *But you also need a plot, you need action,* he would have added, but the taxidermist interrupted him.

"The list grows long. The play is constructed around it. I will read it to you, the full sewing kit list. Virgil reads it out one last time near the end of the play. This list is my greatest literary achievement."

Henry might have laughed at the statement, but the taxidermist just wasn't a man you laughed at or with. The air around him, the expression on his face, sucked the life out of laughter.

The list, exceptionally among the elements of his play, was not found amidst the papers on top of his desk, but was extracted from a drawer. The taxidermist read:

A howl, a black cat, words and occasional silence, a hand gesture, shirts with one arm missing, a prayer, a set speech at the start of every parliamentary session, a song, a food dish, a float in a parade, commemorative porcelain shoes for the people, tennis lessons, plain truth common nouns, onelongword, lists, empty good cheer expressed in extremis, witness words, rituals and pilgrimages, private and public acts of justice and homage, a facial expression, a second hand gesture, a verbal expression, [*sic*] dramas, 68 Nowolipki Street, games for Gustav, a tattoo, an object designated for a year, aukitz.

It was mumbo jumbo. Heard but not read, and heard only once, the words vanishing into silence before he could seize their meaning, Henry retained hardly anything and understood even less. He didn't know how to react, so he said nothing. But the taxidermist wasn't saying anything either.

"I didn't get the last one," Henry said, at length.

"Aukitz, a-u-k-i-t-z."

"It sounds like German, but I don't recognize the word."

"No, it's not. It's a kind of onelongword."

"It doesn't seem that long to me, only six letters."

"No, that's not it."

The taxidermist turned the page and pointed with his finger at a word in the middle of it: onelongword.

"What does it mean?"

"It's one of Beatrice's ideas."

He searched and found:

BEATRICE: I have something.

VIRGIL: What's that?

BEATRICE: One long word. Or rather onelongword, in one word.

VIRGIL: What word exa—

BEATRICE: Shhh!

VIRGIL: (*frightened, in a whisper*) What is it?

BEATRICE: I thought I heard something.

(*Silence.*)

VIRGIL: Well?

BEATRICE: Nothing.

VIRGIL: Are you sure?

BEATRICE: No.

VIRGIL: Should we run?

BEATRICE: In what direction?

VIRGIL: The one opposite from where the noise came from.

BEATRICE: I'm not sure where it came from.

VIRGIL: We're surrounded!

BEATRICE: Shhh, be quiet!

"A scene follows where they think they've been found, but they're wrong. They're still safe. They come back to one-longword."

BEATRICE: Virgil?

(*Virgil has fallen asleep. He slowly falls over until he is resting against Beatrice. He begins to snore gently.*

Beatrice does not move or make a noise. Nor does she fall asleep. She instead looks around. Her vigilance is fearful, but the peace and stillness relax her and she starts to observe the surrounding scenery with thoughtful curiosity.)

BEATRICE: Such a wondrous view.

(*Silence, except for Virgil's snoring.*)

VIRGIL: (*waking up suddenly*) What? What was I saying?

BEATRICE: I don't know. I fell asleep.

VIRGIL: You did?

BEATRICE: I did.

VIRGIL: You're always sleeping.

BEATRICE: Anything to report from your watch?

VIRGIL: (*yawning, stretching and rubbing his eyes*) Nothing to report.

BEATRICE: Good.

VIRGIL: Where were we?

BEATRICE: What do you mean?

VIRGIL: In our discussion. We were talking about talking about the Horrors.

BEATRICE: Onelongword.

VIRGIL: That's right, in one word. So what do you mean by that?

BEATRICE: It would be one long word that, by agreement, would be about the Horrors.

VIRGIL: Do you have one in mind?

BEATRICE: Thepityofitallwhensomuchwaspossible.

VIRGIL: I like it. I have one too.

BEATRICE: Let's hear it.

VIRGIL: Evilivingroomanerroneously.

"Say that one again," Henry said.

VIRGIL: Evilivingroomanerroneously.

BEATRICE: Harder to follow.

The taxidermist nodded, acknowledging that Beatrice and Henry had the same opinion of Virgil's onelongword.

VIRGIL: It's as you said: an agreement, a convention. We
          agree that a onelongword is about the Horrors.
BEATRICE: Agreed.
VIRGIL: Let me write this down. (*He writes on Beatrice's back
          with his fingertip.*)

"Aukitz is a variation on a onelongword. Beatrice pro-
poses that the word be printed in every book, magazine and
newspaper, in a spot conspicuous or discreet, depending on
the wishes of the author or publisher, to indicate that the
language within is knowing of the Horrors."

"And all the other items in the list, this sewing kit for
the Shirt, have the same purpose, to make things knowing?"

"Yes, exactly."

"Can I see the list, please?"

The taxidermist hesitated, but then passed it to Henry.

"Thank you," Henry said, managing to check any out-
ward sign of surprise. He could barely believe it. He was
certain the taxidermist would snatch the page back before
he had time to read it. Finally he would stop the flow of the
taxidermist's words and have them before his eyes, fixed
and immobile, like one of his mounted animals. The words
were lightly indented into the page, creating a Braille-like
embossment on the reverse side, the result of being mechanically typed.

The list was laid out in a column:

A Horrors' Sewing Kit

a howl,

a black cat,

words and occasional silence,

a hand gesture,

shirts with one arm missing,

a prayer,

a set speech at the start of every
    parliamentary session,

a song,

a food dish,

a float in a parade,

commemorative porcelain shoes for the
    people,

tennis lessons,

plain truth common nouns,

onelongword,

lists,

empty good cheer expressed in extremis,

witness words,

rituals and pilgrimages,

private and public acts of justice and
    homage,

a facial expression,

a second hand gesture,

a verbal expression,

[sic] dramas,

```
68 Nowolipki Street,
games for Gustav,
a tattoo,
an object designated for a year,
aukitz.
```

The full stop after the last item had perforated the page. The list had a curious poetry to it, an anti-poetry of the odd and the oddly juxtaposed, of the familiar and the strange. Henry's eyes stopped for a moment on an item towards the end of the list: 68 Nowolipki Street. The address tugged at his memory, but he couldn't tell why. He moved on. Clearly the taxidermist felt very strongly about this list and Henry was expected to ask questions about it. But he sighed inwardly. To tell a story through a *list*. It wouldn't be any more killing to an audience if he sat on a stage and started reading from the phone book. Henry arbitrarily picked an item.

"What are 'plain truth common nouns'?" he asked.

"They're judgments that are backed up by the dictionary. It's Beatrice's idea. So: murderers, killers, exterminators, torturers, plunderers, robbers, rapists, defilers, brutes, louts, monsters, fiends—words like that."

"I get the idea." Henry chose another item from the list. "And this 'verbal expression'?"

The taxidermist found the scene:

BEATRICE: Very well. And you have something else?

    (*Virgil begins his pacing again.*)

VIRGIL: An expression.

BEATRICE: Again? You'll sprain your face.

VIRGIL: I mean a verbal expression. The central section of any group of people—whether seated or standing, whether in a line or in rows and columns—would be designated with the term "in the Horrors". Which is not to be taken in a negative sense necessarily. After all, to be in the middle of a row is to be in the safest spot from the dangers on the edges of the row. So when we are attending a play and we are told by the usher, "You will see best if you sit in the Horrors," or "I'm afraid the Horrors are taken," we will know what is meant, and we'll perhaps remember what happened to others in other circumstances who were "in the Horrors". Shall I continue?

BEATRICE: Please.

The taxidermist stopped.

Henry nodded. "And '[*sic*] dramas'?"

"*Sic* is the Latin word for *thus*," the taxidermist replied. "It's used to indicate that a printed word is printed exactly as intended or is correctly copied from the erroneous original."

"Yes, I'm familiar with the use of *sic*."

"Virgil has this idea for short plays where every word, every single word, would be qualified by *sic*, because every word, in the light of the Horrors, is now erroneous. There's a Hungarian writer who writes like that, in a way."

The taxidermist didn't search for the scene where Virgil presents his [sic] dramas, nor did he tell Henry which Hungarian writer he was referring to. Instead, he fell silent. They seemed to be in an intermission, so to speak. Henry decided to seize the opportunity and try again, but this time from a different angle, from the point of view of character development rather than plot and action. That might help the taxidermist with his play—and get him to talk about its genesis.

"Tell me, how do Beatrice and Virgil change over the course of the play?" Henry asked.

"Change? Why should they change? They have no reason to change. They've done nothing wrong. They're exactly the same at the end of the play as they were at the beginning."

"But they talk. They notice and realize things. They reflect in quiet moments. They gather up the items that go into the sewing kit. All these change them, no?"

"Absolutely not," the taxidermist said firmly. "They're the same. If we had met them the next day, we would have said they were no different from the previous day."

Henry wondered what his creative writing friend would have said at that moment. He had found three good words, more than that, in fact, but no story was coming from them.

"But in a story, the characters—"

"Animals have endured for countless thousands of years. They've been confronted by the most adverse environments imaginable and they've adapted, but in a manner absolutely consistent with their natures."

"That's true in life. I fully agree. I have no doubts about the organic workings of evolution. In a story, however—"

"It is *we* who have to change, not they." The taxidermist seemed flustered.

"I agree with you. There's no future without an environmental conscience. But in a story—here, take Julian in the Flaubert story you sent me. Over the course—"

"If Virgil and Beatrice have to change according to someone else's standards, they might as well give up and be extinct."

At that moment, it was Henry who gave up. "Yes, I see your point," he said, to placate the taxidermist.

"They do not change. Virgil and Beatrice are the same before, during and after."

Henry looked at the list again.

"Where's this '68 Nowolip—'" he was about to ask, to change the topic, but the taxidermist abruptly raised the palm of his hand in the air.

Henry shut up. The taxidermist got up and came round to his side of the desk. Henry felt a slight measure of apprehension.

"Only one thing really counts," said the taxidermist. It was nearly a whisper.

"What's that?"

The taxidermist slowly pulled the page from Henry's hand. Henry let it slide through his fingers. The taxidermist laid it on the desk.

"This," he said.

He took the lamp in one hand and with the other he ran his fingers against the direction of the fur at the base of Virgil's tail.

"This here," he said.

Henry looked. On the skin now exposed was a stitch, a suture, that circled the base of the tail. It looked purple, medical, horrible.

"The tail was cut off," the taxidermist said. "I reattached it."

Henry stared. The taxidermist put the lamp back on the counter and walked over to a table at the far end of the workshop. Henry reached and touched Virgil's fur, meaning to smooth it down, but instead he pushed it back to look again. He didn't know why he did this, but he looked and then he touched. A shudder went through him. He pulled his fingers back and patted the fur down. He felt gutted. How utterly barbarous to do that, to cut Virgil's splendid tail off. Who would do such a thing?

Henry wondered why the taxidermist had stopped telling him about his play. He was standing in front of a table, handling something. Had Henry been too hard on him? Insensitive to his struggles?

"Why don't you let me read your play, or what you have of it?"

The taxidermist didn't answer.

Was it the feeling that he would be revealing the treasure he'd been working on his whole life, and that once it was out, he'd be left empty, without secrets, bereft? Was he afraid of the exposure of his inner self? Of Henry's and other people's reactions? *"Years of work and this is all you have to show for it?"* Was he sensing the failure of his enterprise, for a reason he could not determine and with no solution he could imagine? Henry realized he couldn't answer any of these questions because he had no sense of the taxidermist's inner self. The man, despite the play and the conversations they'd had, remained a mystery to him. Worse: a void.

"I should . . ." Henry began to say, but he trailed off. At every visit, the taxidermist swallowed up so much of his time. He got up and moved to where the man was standing.

He was working on a red fox. It was lying on its back and he'd already made a cut along its stomach, from the lower ribs to the base of the tail. He began to lift the skin off the body, using his fingers and the knife. Henry watched him work with morbid fascination. He'd never seen a freshly dead animal so close up. The taxidermist pulled the skin away until he reached the base of the tail, which he cut from the inside with the knife. Then he worked on the legs until he reached the knee joints, which he cut through. There was little blood. Pale pink—muscle, Henry guessed—and streaks of white—fat—predominated, with only here and there spots and patches of deep purple. Henry thought the taxidermist would now continue upwards with the ventral cut, to the base of the neck, slicing the chest area open and doing there to the front legs what he had done lower down to the back ones. Instead the taxidermist started turning the animal's skin inside out, easing the body through the ventral cut, separating skin from body with the knife as he went along. The skin was coming off the animal like a pullover. When he reached the front legs, he severed the legs at the shoulders and continued peeling the animal's skin off the neck. At the head, he cut where the ears were attached to the skull. Two dark holes were left behind. The eyes were a weirder sight. Whereas the fox's ears, their outer structure, went with the skin, the eyes remained behind, staring out even more now for having their eyelids removed. The taxidermist artfully cut the only place in the eyes where skin and body were linked: the tear ducts. Then the mouth was released, the blade cutting through the skin next to the gums. Lastly, the nose, the final point of attachment, was dealt with, the black skin skinned off and the cartilage cut through. He returned the skin to its natural shape, inside in, and there they lay, side by side, the skin and the flayed carcass, like a baby that has been taken out of its red pyjamas, only a baby fiercely staring with the blackest eyes and displaying a full set of teeth.

"I've done this for you," the taxidermist said. "It's a head mount. All I need is the head."

He picked up a scalpel and made a small cut at the base of the fox skin's throat. Then, with a pair of small, sharp scissors, making sure not to cut through fur, but only through the skin at its base, he cut the fox's skull-less head off. He turned the head inside out again, including the ears. Picking with his fingers and scraping with the side of the knife, he cleaned flesh and fat off the skin.

"Need to treat it," he muttered. He walked over to a shelf of jars.

Henry stared at the head. It was a fox's head, but emptied and turned inside out. A snout, a mouth, eyes, large ears, a neck—but all wrong, all inside out. Henry could see white fur inside the mouth, where a tongue should have been, and at the neck cut he could see red fur bursting out. The rest was the peeled head, pink and raw, of a formerly sentient being. The ears, despite being the largest features, were inexpressive. But the eyes, the eyelids rather, were closed, while the mouth was open, as if in a scream. He looked at the neck cut again, at the red fur emerging from within. *A soul on fire*, he thought. The head suddenly became that of a being caught in its moment of greatest agony, shuddering uncontrollably, beyond reason and beyond help. A feeling of horror overcame Henry.

The taxidermist came back with a small pot of white paste, quite granular. "Borax," he said, without further explanation.

With one hand inside the fox's head and the other wearing a rubber glove, he began to apply the paste to the animal's head, rubbing it in vigorously.

"I have to go," Henry said. "I'll come back again soon."

The taxidermist said nothing. It was as if Henry weren't even there. Henry turned, left the workshop, picked up the end of Erasmus's leash, and walked out into the late afternoon.

The next weeks were some of the most intense and chaotic Henry had ever known in his life.

The Greenhouse Players were in the run-up to their next play, one in which Henry was reaching his modest acme as an actor. He was playing the lead role in Lessing's *Nathan the Wise.*

The Greenhouse Players had existed for more than twenty years as local purveyors of broad farces when a new director came on board and transformed the company. In a stroke, the coarse, the facile and the conventional were banned. "Why leave all the good stuff to the professionals?" he asked. "Great theatre is for everyone." That greatness could be seen as much in the flawed attempt as in the polished success, he argued. It was a potential recipe for disaster, and indeed there were surely, in the early days, shows that were more fun for the players than for the spectators. But what was the risk? Everyone participating did it for nothing, for the simple joy of being theatrically creative.

The director was an old Serbian immigrant—he called himself a Yugoslav—and he was animated by an unwavering faith in the dignity and equality of all, a positive relic of communism. He had a vision and he pursued it. He possessed the unerring ability to find the actor in each person he directed, with the point being not to erase the person behind the role but to merge person and role, so that they were balanced. "Don't worry about being good," he used to tell the troupe. "Aspire to be authentic." Casting was entirely age-blind, colour-blind, accent-blind, body-shape-blind and, when it was not directly relevant, gender-blind. This was theatre of the people, by the people, for the people. It had to be seen to be appreciated.

Under his firm yet fair guidance, the Greenhouse Players rose in the world's—that is, the city's—estimation. The widely read weekly city entertainment magazine had once done a feature on the Players—"Exalted Amateurism," the piece was titled—and they regularly attracted the notice of community media. All agreed that it was a serious endeavour and a fascinating, ongoing sociological experiment. As a result of the publicity, the spectator base had expanded to include a good number of university students—as much of sociology and cultural studies as of literature—as well as theatre lovers and the usual suspects of family and friends.

These developments all took place before Henry's time; the Greenhouse Players were already well established when he joined the troupe. They were one of the reasons he didn't want to leave the city. He loved sitting in a circle of chairs on a bare stage with fellow actors as they worked their way through a script. The trust, the fraternity, the joy!

Henry was very focussed on the upcoming production. But he did not forget the taxidermist. His thoughts regularly returned to animals and the "irreparable abomination" being done to them and the drama the taxidermist wanted to make of it.

Henry and Sarah had their own reasons to dwell on the suffering of animals. Henry came home one day and was surprised not to be greeted by Mendelssohn, their cat. She normally appeared at the end of the hallway when she heard the door open, her tail raised in the air shaped like a question mark. Nor did Erasmus show up, sniffing wildly. Sarah was sleeping—and a pregnant woman's sleep is sacred— so Henry quietly went looking for Mendelssohn. He looked under the sofa, which was her normal refuge. She wasn't there. Finally it was a smear of blood near a bookshelf that led him to her. She had jammed herself between the floor and the lowest shelf. Henry clucked and called her name in a whisper. She gave out the feeblest meow. When she crawled out, her nose was dripping blood and her back was covered in it, the skin torn and the fur matted, and she didn't seem able to stand on her back legs. Since she was a house cat, barring a freak accident, there was only one possible source of the injury: Erasmus. That answered Henry's question about how they would get along (but they *did* get along for the longest time, and why shouldn't they?).

Erasmus had been behaving a little strangely recently, Sarah and he had noticed. Henry turned his head and saw Erasmus across the room. The dog wasn't right; Henry could see that straightaway. And it wasn't feelings of guilt at attacking Mendelssohn or anxiety at the prospect of punishment. It was something else. Henry called him three times in a gentle voice. Erasmus wouldn't come. When Henry got closer, the dog growled. Suspecting something might be wrong, Henry put on a coat and thick gloves and caught the dog. Erasmus put up a raging fight, snarling and barking as he'd never done before. Sarah woke up screaming. Henry yelled at her not to come out of the bedroom. He noticed that Erasmus had scratch marks on his face; Mendelssohn had defended herself. When Henry had the dog wrapped in a towel in a chokehold, he called out to Sarah. She gathered up poor Mendelssohn and put her in her travelling case.

Henry hauled the two animals to the vet in a taxi. Sarah wanted to come, but they agreed that in view of her pregnant condition and the dog's strange behaviour, it was best if she stayed home.

How their dog, who was supposed to have been vaccinated, caught *rabies*, which turned out to be the diagnosis, was a question that neither the vet nor the shelter where they had got him could answer. There are all kinds of wild animals in big cities that have rabies, he was told. Worse even: the plague. But proper sanitary conditions prevent the spread of these diseases and they don't normally jump to pets. Perhaps the vaccine had failed. Henry wondered if Erasmus could have contracted rabies at the taxidermist's store. The notion was ridiculous; nonetheless, it trotted in his head.

Mendelssohn's back was broken and her lungs punctured, clearly as a result of a bite by Erasmus. She was in great pain and she had to be put down. One of her forepaws was shaved and while Henry held her on the table, the vet pricked the bald patch of skin with the needle. She didn't struggle. She was trusting. The instant the vet pressed on the syringe plunger, the light went out in Mendelssohn's eyes and her head fell forward.

Erasmus's end was a harsher affair. In the frenzied state the dog was in, Henry was told to release him into a large sealed box that had a window. The vet's exact diagnosis came later, after an autopsy. The initial one, the one that sealed Erasmus's fate, was based on a visual inspection through that window. Erasmus was at first violently frantic, barking and growling and hurling his snout against the window, trying to bite observers through it, completely un-recognizable in character, but after a while he curled up on the floor like his old self, only trembling and whimpering. The slight wheezing sound of the gas set him off again. He jumped up in a last mad lunge of anger. But the gas was quick, though not as quick as Mendelssohn's needle prick, and he fell over, mouth frothing, eyes rolling and legs trem-bling. By the time Henry was allowed to hold him again, Erasmus was completely stiff.

Henry managed to hold it together at the clinic. He was alone among strangers, there was a procedure to follow to establish a diagnosis, there were decisions to be made, a bill to be paid. In the taxi back home, he just stared out the win-dow, numb. It was climbing the stairs to their apartment, feeling the emptiness at his feet where normally there would have been a dog, feeling the emptiness of his right hand where normally there would have been a leash, that he broke down. It took him long minutes before he could put the key in the door and let himself in. He was dreading having to tell Sarah what had happened. She was carrying a life within herself, and sensitive to life, worried about life.

Sarah was standing in the hallway, right where Mendelssohn used to stand, waiting for him, eyes open wide, anxious. But he didn't need to say anything. She saw right away the emptiness he brought back, the dramatic absence of life.

They both burst into tears. She'd returned exhausted from visiting a friend, she blubbered, and had gone straight to bed. Next she knew, Erasmus was barking furiously and Henry was shouting at her to stay in the bedroom. She hadn't noticed anything unusual with the animals when she'd returned home, but nor had she sought them out. She couldn't remember if she'd even seen Mendelssohn. She was too tired; she'd just wanted to have her nap. Maybe Erasmus hadn't attacked Mendelssohn yet. She blamed herself for not looking for her. Henry blamed himself for not taking proper note of Erasmus's character change, a sullenness that had not been there before.

Then there was the worry of having caught the disease themselves. Sarah was terrified of losing the baby, but Henry did most of the animal care and she was positive that she hadn't been bitten or even scratched by either Erasmus or Mendelssohn. Henry was sure he hadn't either, but since he had handled them in their last hours, he received a course of rabies vaccine shots.

One evening, a fellow actor from the play came up to him before rehearsal.

"Henry," he said, "I didn't know you were a famous writer. I thought you were just a waiter in a café."

He was speaking as if in jest, this hotshot lawyer actor friend, but Henry could tell his intent was serious. He was saying, *Who are you? What is your standing in society? I thought I knew you, but apparently I don't.* Was there resentment in his tone? Was Henry to be treated differently now? Was there something wrong in Henry having let a part of his identity remain unknown?

"Some guy was looking for you last time," continued the lawyer. "You'd already left. He said he knew you and kept on describing you but with the wrong name. He finally showed me the picture from the newspaper."

There'd been a photo from a rehearsal and a short article in the city paper the previous week. In spite of the makeup and the costume, and though his name was not given, Henry was clearly recognizable in it.

Henry had an inkling. "What was his name? Was he tall, older, very serious?"

"He wouldn't give his name. But that's him. As serious as an undertaker. You know him?"

"Yes, I know him."

"He had this for you," the lawyer said, handing Henry an envelope.

The envelope confirmed that it had indeed been the taxidermist. Why wouldn't he give his name? Henry wondered. He puzzled at the man's paranoia and secrecy. It hadn't occurred to him that the taxidermist didn't know his real name. Each time they'd seen each other, it was just the two of them and there had been no need to use names, real or fictitious.

The envelope contained another scene from the taxidermist's play:

BEATRICE: I've had enough of lists.

VIRGIL: So have I.

(*Beatrice sighs, lays her head down and falls asleep. Virgil wanders off. In the bushes he finds a large piece of cloth, bright red and patternless. Is it a tablecloth? A bolt of fabric? Virgil picks it up and plays with it. He waves it about. Throws it in the air and watches it fall. Wraps himself in it. Then he falls back and starts wrestling with it, the red cloth above him and he on the ground on his back. Suddenly he stops and turns to the audience.*)

VIRGIL: Someone is dying and as they are dying they grab at the red cloth of suffering and they pull and tear at it and nothing before in their life has involved them so completely emotionally or overwhelmed them with such crushing intellectual totality—"I'm dying, I'm dying!"—so the cloth becomes everything they see

and feel, covering the walls and ceiling of their room
or, if they're dying in the open, filling the entire
dome of the sky, but getting closer by the minute
until the red cloth of suffering clings to their body
like clothing, only tighter, then clings like a shroud,
only tighter, then clings like embalming bands, only
tighter, until the red cloth chokes them and they
breathe their last, at which moment the cloth, as if
pulled by a magician, vanishes and there is only a
body left, surrounded by people whose very pulsing
being has made them incapable of seeing the cloth,
and life goes on, triumphant, one might say, until the
day the red cloth flutters into your view and you
realize it's coming your way and you wonder, with
utter disbelief, how you could have missed seeing it
before, how you could have ignored it, but your
contemplations are cut short because you've already
fallen back and started wrestling with the red cloth
of suffering, pulling and tearing at it.

(*He wrestles with the red cloth.*)

BEATRICE: (*waking up*) What are you doing?

VIRGIL: (*stopping instantly*) Nothing. Just folding this piece of
cloth.

(*He folds the cloth into a neat rectangle and puts it
down.*)

BEATRICE: Where did you find it?

VIRGIL: (*pointing*) There.

BEATRICE: I wonder how it got there?

VIRGIL: I don't know.

(*Silence.*)

VIRGIL: We could do with a little good cheer.

BEATRICE: We could.

VIRGIL: Something funny.

BEATRICE: Something very funny.

VIRGIL: But not empty good cheer.

BEATRICE: No.

VIRGIL: Although better empty good cheer than no cheer at all.

BEATRICE: I don't think so. The contrast between despair and empty good cheer would only make the despair worse.

VIRGIL: But if empty good cheer were expressed in extremis, might the irony of it not push one to transcend despair and bring on genuine good cheer? At that critical moment, might empty good cheer not be the first rung on a philosophical ladder to complete cosmic realization?

BEATRICE: It's a remote possibility.

VIRGIL: Why don't we try it? Why don't we agree to fall into empty good cheer when we are truly desperate, as a last resort?

BEATRICE: We can try.

VIRGIL: But are we truly desperate at this moment?

BEATRICE: (*with a trace of good cheer*) No, we're not.

VIRGIL: (*cheerily*) One rung up! I'll write it down. (*He writes on Beatrice's back with his fingertip.*)

Henry looked over Virgil's soliloquy a second time. It was a single long sentence. He could imagine an actor getting into it, the energy building. The change of pronouns was effective, from "someone" and "they" to "you", hinging on "one" in the ironic "life goes on, triumphant, one might say." He remembered the "empty good cheer expressed in extremis" from the sewing kit. A typed note accompanied the scene. It was in the taxidermist's typical laconic style:

```
My story has no story.
It rests on the fact of murder.
```

There was neither salutation nor sign-off. Henry tried to figure out why the taxidermist had sent him that particular scene with this note. The red cloth of suffering—was that a sign of the taxidermist's own anxiety? As for the empty good cheer—was it a signal that he needed help, that he himself was feeling in extremis? Henry determined to go see him again soon.

Once Henry's "secret identity" was outed, relations with his fellow amateur actors weren't quite the same. Though Henry was exactly the same person he had been at the last rehearsal, he could tell that his fellow actors were looking at him differently. In conversations he was interrupted less often, perhaps, but he was also included less often. The director became alternately too hard on him or too soft. It was nothing unmanageable. Time and renewed familiarity would even things out once more. But it was a little stressful in the immediate run-up to an opening.

His music teacher knew. In the course of conversations before and after lessons, it had come out. His teacher had slapped his forehead and smiled. He'd read Henry's famous book. His daughter had offered it to him. He was proud of Henry, which was nice, and then during lessons he was exactly the same as he was before—except for the change in metaphors. Nothing so domestic as an ox anymore. Henry's clarinet was now a wild animal that needed taming.

Nathan the Wise opened with the usual mad rush to get everything ready in time, with the usual jitters, with the usual slipups, all accepted and forgiven in the name of "authenticity". The play ran Thursday to Sunday two weeks in a row and it went well, although one can never tell about a play in which one is a participant because one never sees the play oneself. The community press, at least, was positive.

And then Sarah's water broke. She heaved to the horizontal. Soon she was racked by contractions. They headed for the hospital. Over the course of the next twenty-four hours, she was reduced to a mucky animal who, after many pants, whimpers and screams, excreted from her body a pound of flesh, as the expression goes, that was red, wrinkled and slimy. The event couldn't have been more animal-like if the two of them had been in a muddy pen grunting. The thing produced, weakly gesticulating, looked half-simian, half-alien. Yet the call to Henry's humanity couldn't have been louder or more radical. He couldn't take his eyes off the baby. My son, my son Theo, thought Henry, dumb-founded.

Still, between the dying of Erasmus and Mendelssohn and the playing of Nathan the Wise and the arrival of Theo, Henry thought of the taxidermist and of his play. Something about his creative struggle heartened him. Even if their situations as writers could not be compared, here was a fellow Hephaestus struggling at the smithy.

And Henry thought of the taxidermist for another reason too, because one night his suspicions about the real subject matter of the play were confirmed.

It happened in the middle of the night, one frequently interrupted, as was the new routine, by Theo crying. The dislocations caused by the intense grief, stress and joy of the last weeks no doubt played a role. Whatever the psychological explanation, Henry was sleeping the sleep of the sleep-deprived when the name emerged in his head. It emerged so forcefully that it punctured his sleep and he sat up and awoke at the same moment, crying out: "Emmanuel Ringelblum!"

He stumbled to the computer and in a stupor of fatigue looked through his old flip-book essay. He found the reference to Ringelblum, but not the address. Next he searched through his research files, also on the computer. There too, with more details, he found what he had written on Ringelblum, but once again he had not noted the address. Finally he found it where he should have looked first, on the Internet, which is a net indeed, one that can be cast farther than the eye can see and be retrieved no matter how heavy the haul, its magical mesh never breaking under the strain but always bringing in the most amazing catch. He typed "68 Nowolipki Street" in a search engine and there, in four tenths of a second, he had his answer.

The very next day, unshaven, dishevelled, exhausted, looking like a homeless man, he returned to Okapi Taxidermy. He brought with him all he had of the taxidermist's play, which wasn't much, just the pear scene, the scene Henry had written describing Virgil's howl, and the scene the taxidermist had dropped off at the theatre, about the red cloth of suffering and the empty good cheer. Henry didn't know why he brought these along. Perhaps in his mind he meant to put everything on the table and start all over with the man.

As he approached the store, Henry thought about the taxidermist's note:

```
My story has no story.
It rests on the fact of murder.
```

The murder of whom?

The okapi surprised and delighted him as much as it had the first time. He opened the door to the store and heard the familiar tinkle of the bell. The marvellous cavern of animals opened up. Henry's throat constricted and tears welled in his eyes as he thought of Erasmus and Mendelssohn. It occurred to him that it had never crossed his mind to have them mounted. After a last look and a last hug, he had accepted the disappearance of their bodies.

The taxidermist appeared with his usual swiftness. He stood stock-still, looked hard at Henry, and then disappeared back into his workshop without saying a word. Henry stared in disbelief at the space where the taxidermist had been. He was no more than an acquaintance. True, they had discussed the taxidermist's creative effort, and discussed it at some length—but did that fact mean the elementary rules of good manners were suspended? Perhaps in the taxidermist's mind, having entered the intimacy of his play, Henry had become like family, to be treated with that gruffness we reserve for those to whom we are closest. Henry chose to take the taxidermist's behaviour in this light. Despite his tiredness, he was buoyed by his state as a new father, and he was softened by the thoughts he had just had about Erasmus and Mendelssohn. Henry was in no mood for friction. He took a deep breath and entered the workshop.

The taxidermist was at his desk, looking at his disorganized papers. Henry took his usual place on the stool.

"So what's your real name? What else are you hiding?" the taxidermist said gruffly, without looking up.

Henry answered softly. "My name is Henry L'Hôte. I

write under a pen name. I'm sorry I haven't come to see you in a while. I've been very busy. My son was born. And Erasmus, my dog, you remember? We had to put him down."

How odd, Henry thought, I'm apologizing for the birth of my son and the death of my dog. The taxidermist did not respond. Henry wondered if the man was angry or hurt. He couldn't tell. He had no right either way, Henry knew. He owed the taxidermist nothing. But he had been lucky as an artist and the taxidermist hadn't been. He was stewing over a play that didn't work, while Henry was a new father who happily lived off a novel that did. What would he gain by taking offence at an old man who was miserable?

Henry spoke again. "In your Horrors' sewing kit, you have '68 Nowolipki Street'. Where is that?"

"It's an imaginary address where every trace of the Horrors would be filed away and saved, every memoir, account and history, every photograph and film, every poem and novel, everything. They would all be found at 68 Nowolipki Street."

"And where is 68 Nowolipki Street?"

"In a corner of every mind and on a plaque in every city. It's a symbol, one of Beatrice's ideas."

"Why Nowolipki? Why that strange word?"

"Beatrice felt like crying and she thought, 'Now, oh lip, keep from trembling,' and she shortened it."

"And on Now-oh-lip-keep-from-trembling Street, why number 68?"

"No reason. Just a number I chose."

The taxidermist was being duplicitous. Nowolipki Street was—and is—a street in Warsaw, and 68 Nowolipki Street is the address at which, after the Second World War, ten metal containers and two milk cans were found stuffed with archival material. The material was varied, consisting of studies, testimonies, charts, photographs, drawings, watercolours and underground press clippings, in addition to official documents such as decrees, posters, food rationing cards, identity papers and so on. This vast documentation proved to be a chronicle of every aspect of life and programmed death in the Warsaw Ghetto from 1940 until its elimination in 1943 after the Ghetto Uprising. The material was brought together by a collective of historians, economists, doctors, scientists, rabbis, social workers and others under the leadership of the historian Emmanuel Ringelblum. The group gave itself the code name Oneg Shabbat, which means "Joy of the Sabbath" in Hebrew, because they usually met on Saturdays. The great majority of them perished in the Ghetto or in the aftermath of its destruction.

It was in remembering that address and those desperate time capsules that Henry knew for certain what the taxidermist was doing. Here was irrefutable proof that he was using the Holocaust to speak of the extermination of animal life. Doomed creatures that could not speak for themselves were being given the voice of a most articulate people who had been similarly doomed. He was seeing the tragic fate of animals through the tragic fate of Jews. The Holocaust as allegory. Hence, Virgil's and Beatrice's incessant hunger and fear, their inability to decide where to go or what to do. And when Henry remembered the drawing the taxidermist had shown him with the Horrors hand gesture, it was not what Virgil did with his fingers once his hand was right in front of his chest that struck Henry now—it was the initial position of the arm: something very close to a Hitler salute, wasn't it?

Fate had brought Henry into contact with a writer— well, a struggling writer—who was doing exactly what Henry had argued should be done in his rejected book three years earlier: he was representing the Holocaust differently.

"Why don't you read me another scene from your play? Let's start that way," Henry said.

The taxidermist nodded without saying a word. He found a handful of papers and cleared his throat. In his measured voice he started:

BEATRICE: I never did tell you what happened to me, did I?

VIRGIL: What? When?

BEATRICE: When they arrested me.

VIRGIL: (*uneasy*) No, you didn't. I never asked.

BEATRICE: Would you like to hear about it?

VIRGIL: Only if you want me to.

BEATRICE: I should tell one person at least, so that the experience doesn't vanish without having been put into words. And who else but you?

(*Pause.*)

BEATRICE: I remember the first slap, just as I was being

brought in. Already then something was lost forever, a basic trust. If there's an exquisite collection of Meissen porcelain and a man takes a cup and deliberately drops it to the floor, shattering it, why wouldn't he then proceed to break everything else? What difference does it make, cup or tureen, once the man has made clear his disregard for porcelain? With that first blow, something akin to porcelain shattered in me. It was a hard slap, forceful yet casual, given for no reason, before I had even identified myself. If they would do that to me, why wouldn't they do worse? Indeed, how could they stop themselves? A single blow is a dot, meaningless. It's a line that is wanted, a connection between the dots that will give purpose and direction. One blow demands a second and then a third and onwards.

I was walked down a corridor. I thought I was being brought to a cell. All the doors giving onto it were closed, except for one, which cast a trapezoid of light upon the floor. "Here it comes," a young man at my side said in an offhand tone, as if we were waiting for a bus. He had already taken his jacket off and was rolling up his sleeves. He was a tall, raw-boned man. With him were two other men. They followed his orders. I was brought into a plain, brightly lit room with a bathtub at its centre. The tub was full of water. Without any ado, they pushed me up to it, my body perpendicular to its edge, and they brought me to my knees. They forced my head underwater and kept it there. They didn't have an easy time of it, though. My neck is strong and it was taking all three of them to hold my head down, especially as I kept shoving them aside with my shoulders.

They found a solution: they stood me up, tied my front legs together, tied my back legs together, brought me alongside the bathtub, and pushed me over sideways into it. My legs went flying and I landed on my back with a splash, hitting my head against the tub's edge. They filled the tub with more water. The water was cold, but I soon forgot about that. I struggled, only now they had it easy. One man held my back legs in the air, another held my front legs, and the third was free to push my head back into the water. To be drowning standing up, solid on your four legs, your head set as if you were drinking, is one thing. It's simple drowning, horrible, but at least respectful of your sense of gravity and suited to how your head likes to be positioned. You have a degree of control over when you breathe in the water. But to be on your back, a palm pushing against your jaw, forcing your head backwards into the water, now the water invades your nose right away and you instantly feel you're drowning. Your neck is killing you because you're desperately trying to tilt your head forward. Each time you try to swallow, it's like a knife is piercing your throat. The panic, the terror of it—I had never known anything like it.

I coughed and coughed whenever they let my head out, but before I could get a good breath in, they shoved my head back into the water. The more I struggled, the more they held me down. Quickly I breathed in water and I felt my body suddenly slacken. I thought, *This is death*, which is when they stopped, expertly. They pulled me out and dropped me to the floor. I coughed and vomited water and lay there. I thought my ordeal was over.

It had just begun. They untied my front legs. With slaps and kicks and pulling on my tail, they hauled me up. My back legs were still tied together. Grabbing me by the mane, they directed me to an adjacent room. I hopped along as best I could. I was placed in a stall of sorts and strapped into a harness that ran beneath my chest and held the front of my body up. My front feet stood on a makeshift floor made of rough wood, quite discoloured. One man locked his arm around my head and another kicked my left knee from behind and lifted the foot off the ground, as if he were a blacksmith about to examine my hoof. But he just held my foot in the air. Then the young man knelt down, crowding around my right leg, and he swiftly drove a long nail into the foot that was on the floor. He started just above the rim of the hoof, at an angle to go deep, and he went right through, solidly nailing my foot to the wooden floor. I can still see the hammer going up and down, the man's arm and the top of his head, the swirl of his crown. At every bang of the hammer, a tremor shook my entire body. A pool of blood expanded around my foot. The three men let go and disappeared behind me. They grabbed my tail. It made me shudder, to have six unfriendly hands taking hold of me like that. They began to pull my tail with all their might, starting a tug-of-war between my tail and my hoof.

I brayed and bucked and attempted to kick. But one front leg was nailed to the floor and my back legs were tied together, easily controlled. I had only one front leg free. They kept pulling and pulling. During those seconds of supreme pain, I tilted from being terrified of death to wanting it more than anything else. I wanted to scurry like a rat into darkness and have it over with. I lost consciousness.

It's so hard to talk about it. It hurt, it was painful—that's all there is to say about it, really. But to feel it! We recoil from the flame of a single match, and here I was in the middle of a blaze. And still it wasn't over. When I awoke I saw that my hoof had given out. It had torn off completely. I thought that my pain could go no further, that surely after what I

had just endured there would be no more. There
was. They twisted my head and poured boiling
water into my right ear. They forced a cold iron bar
into my rectum and left it there to chill my innards.
They repeatedly kicked me in the stomach and
genital area. This, over the course of some hours,
taking regular cigarette breaks as I lay helpless in
the harness, sometimes leaving me alone with the
door onto the corridor left open, at other times
standing near me but going on as if I weren't there.
I lost consciousness a number of times.

They insulted me repeatedly, though I wouldn't
say they were actually angry or worked up. They
were just doing their job. When they got tired, they
worked in silence.

It ended in the late afternoon, around five o'clock,
I suppose, after a day's work was done. Home
beckoned. They unstrapped me from the harness
and threw me into a small cell. After two days and
nights of solitary confinement, pain-ridden and
foodless, I was released. They opened my cell door,
stood me up, marched me out, and left me at the
outside gate. Not a word was said. I didn't know
where you were and you didn't know where I was. I
limped away until I reached the riverbank, where I
collapsed in a secluded spot and where you
eventually found me.

VIRGIL: I asked around. I was afraid my questions would

arouse suspicion. I was afraid I would be taken in. But I had to find you. Finally, I went to where you used to work. The family had turned you out and didn't know where you were, but a servant came out as I was leaving and told me that she'd heard from someone who'd heard from someone that you had been taken to such-and-such police station. I went to the station, made cautious inquiries, and from there fanned out, looking under bridges, down alleys, behind bushes, until I came upon you.

BEATRICE: The first place where you touched me was my neck.

VIRGIL: Yes, I remember.

BEATRICE: There.

VIRGIL: There.

BEATRICE: Your soft, small hand.

VIRGIL: Your soft, warm neck.

(*They weep.*
Beatrice falls asleep.
Silence.)

The silence in the play continued out of it. The taxidermist didn't say anything more and Henry was speechless. It wasn't just the elaborate, institutional torturing of a donkey. It was something else that arrested him, a detail about the head torturer. Beatrice described him as "a tall, raw-boned man". The second adjective was unusual enough that for a moment Henry misunderstood it; a literal and gruesome image flitted through his mind. Then he remembered its proper meaning: lean, gaunt, an absence of fleshiness. Henry dwelt on the image. A tall, raw-boned man. He glanced at the taxidermist. Perhaps it was a coincidence.

"Well, that was disturbing," Henry finally said.

The taxidermist did not reply.

"Among the characters in the play, you mention a boy and his two friends. When do they appear?" Henry asked.

"At the very end of the play."

"There's this sudden intrusion of human characters in your animal allegory."

"That's right." The taxidermist said nothing more, only looked out blankly.

"What happens with the boy?"

The taxidermist picked up some papers.

"Virgil has just finished reading out the sewing kit as they have it so far. You remember the sewing kit?"

"I do."

He read:

BEATRICE: That's a good start.

VIRGIL: I think so.

(*Silence.*)

VIRGIL: The Horrors is a dirty shirt that needs washing.

BEATRICE: A very dirty shirt.

(*Silence.*

Noise to one side.)

THE BOY: (*pushing through bushes and emerging, a rifle in one hand, taken aback to see Virgil and Beatrice*) What?

(*His two friends appear behind him. Virgil and Beatrice rise to their feet and stand pressed together.*

All freeze. Virgil's hairs are standing on end. Beatrice's ears are flat against her skull. They are too frightened to move, besides being weak from hunger.)

"They recognize the boy," the taxidermist interrupted. "The day before, in the village where they were staying, this boy had been one of the main instigators in some terrible deeds."

"Go on," Henry said.

The taxidermist read:

THE BOY: (*the initial shyness gone, smiling*) Wait. (*He wags a finger.*) I recognize you. I've seen you before. (*He laughs.*) Where did you go? How come you disappeared? (*He moves closer, a swagger to his walk. To his friends.*) I recognize them. (*To Virgil and Beatrice.*) We're heading that way. There's more work to be done, if you know what I mean. (*The same natural, jaunty walk, the same smile as yesterday in the village. His two friends begin playing the game, circling the two animals with mock casualness.*) Do you know what I mean?

VIRGIL: (*to Beatrice, desperately*) Beatrice, Beatrice, do you remember? A black cat and tennis lessons. Let us hide in the Horrors, several rows in. And remember: empty good cheer expressed in extremis. Not a moment to be lost. Be happy right now. Be happy. I'm so happy with you, so very happy. Let us dance with our porcelain shoes. Everything will be all right. I'm smiling and laughing and happy. I'm full of joy [*sic! sic! sic!*]. (*All the while, he is gliding his hand through the air in front of his chest, pointing two fingers down and then dropping his hand, repeating the gesture over and over—he's doing the first Horrors hand gesture.*)

THE BOY: What are you babbling about, you crazy old monkey?

BEATRICE: (*in a quavering voice*) Y-yes! I'm ha-happy too. I'm very happy.

THE BOY: I'm glad to hear it.

(*In one smooth motion, the Boy swings his rifle and strikes Virgil hard across the head with its butt. Virgil is not expecting the blow and makes no attempt to deflect it. There is a cracking sound. Virgil produces a startled exhalation and falls over. Beatrice shouts and collapses. Already the left part of Virgil's frontal bone is smashed and the frontal lobe damaged, which results in cerebral haemorrhaging. Virgil desperately tries to cling to consciousness and to keep hold of Beatrice's body, but he is sinking fast. The Boy's further blows with the rifle butt are superfluous. Severe injuries are inflicted to Virgil's face, notably the breaking of the jaw and left cheekbone, the breaking of several of the upper and lower teeth, and the bursting of the right eyeball. Several ribs on his right*)

*side are broken, as is the femur of his right leg. The loss of
consciousness is quickly followed by death.*

*Beatrice is held down and beaten with the rifle butt
and kicked. While this is happening, she tries to reach
Virgil with a hoof and she shouts that she is happy with
Virgil, very happy, and that the Horrors is a dirty shirt
that needs washing, and she searches for another word,
her own word, a onelongword; she finally shouts,
"Aukitz!" but then falls into a silent blankness of pain
and terror.*

*When they let her go, she manages to stretch and touch
Virgil's body. She is shot three times, one bullet lodging
itself in her shoulder, one entering and exiting her body
through the chest area, coming close to the heart, and the
last entering her head through the left eye orbit and lodging
itself in her brain, which is the direct cause of death.*

*The Boy, in passing, notices the odd markings on
Beatrice's back. He runs his hands over them, prompted as
much by a desire to inspect as to ruin.*

*The Boy produces a small knife and cuts Virgil's tail
off. He flicks the soft tail in the air like a whip as he and
his friends move away. After a short distance, he carelessly
tosses the tail to the ground.)*

The taxidermist fell silent.

"And that's how the play ends?" Henry said.

"That's how the play ends. After that, the curtain comes
down."

The taxidermist got up and walked to one of the counters. After a moment Henry followed him. The taxidermist was looking at some pages he'd neatly spread out.

"What's this?" Henry asked.

"A scene I'm working on."

"What's it about?"

"Gustav."

"Who's Gustav?"

"He's a dead, naked body that's been lying near Virgil and Beatrice's tree the whole time."

"A *human* body? Another human?"

"Yes."

"Lying in the open?"

"No, in some bushes. Virgil discovers him."

"They don't smell his body before that?"

"Sometimes life stinks just as much as death. They don't."

"How do they know he's called Gustav?"

"They don't. Virgil calls him that to give him a name."

"Why is he naked?"

"They figure he was told to strip and was then shot. They think the red cloth was probably his. He might have been a peddler."

"Why do they stay? After finding a dead body, wouldn't the more natural reaction be to run away?"

"They think of it as a place already plundered and now safe."

"What do they do about Gustav? Do they bury him?"

"No, they play games."

"*Games?*"

"Yes. It's another way they find of talking about the Horrors. It's in the sewing kit."

That's right, Henry remembered: games for Gustav.

"Isn't that an odd thing to do, to play games when there's a dead body right next to you?" Henry said.

"They imagine that Gustav would enjoy them if he were still alive. Playing games is a way of celebrating life."

"What kind of games?"

"That was my question for you. I thought you might come up with a few. You seem like the playful sort."

"What, like hide-and-seek?"

"I was hoping for something more sophisticated."

"You mentioned some terrible deeds instigated by the boy who kills Beatrice and Virgil."

"Yes."

"Beatrice and Virgil saw these deeds?"

"Yes."

"What did they see?"

The taxidermist said nothing. Henry was about to repeat his question but he thought better of it. He waited. After a long while, the taxidermist spoke.

"At first they didn't see. They heard. They were standing by the village pond among some bushes, sipping at the water's edge, when they heard screams. They looked up and saw two young women wearing long skirts and heavy peasant boots running for the pond, clutching bundles to their chests. Some men were behind them, not in hot pursuit but rather seeming to enjoy the women's flight. Terror and the grimmest determination were written on the women's faces. First one reached the pond, then the other. Both ran into it without a pause. When they were thigh-deep in the water, they dropped what they were carrying.

"It was then that Virgil and Beatrice saw that their bundles were swaddled babies. The women pushed their babies underwater and held them there. Even after the few bubbles stopped popping at the surface, there was no hesitation on their part, no flexing of the arms. On the contrary, the women continued to move deeper into the pond, kicking at their skirts and losing and regaining their footing. The men lining the edge of the pond—there must have been ten or so—far from offering any kind of help, jeered the women on.

"When she was certain that her baby could no longer be alive, yet still clutching it beneath the surface, one of the women, now past her waist in the black water, plunged headfirst and immediately was drowned. Neither she nor her baby broke the surface again. They both sank to the bottom. The other woman tried to do the same but could not manage it, even when it was obvious that her baby, like the other, was dead. She kept coming up for air, coughing and snorting, which provoked laughter among the men, who shouted advice on how best to drown. Whereas the first woman's death had proceeded with the swiftness of gravity, the second woman's took longer. For minutes she stood in the water, shivering and staring at its surface and looking at the men on the shore and attempting again to drown herself, all done without any show or any effort to communicate, only with the grave look of someone trying to kill herself. Her baby was gone and she was determined to follow it close behind. Finally, with a glance up to the sky, lifting the soggy mass of her baby out of the water and pressing it to her chest, the woman forcefully threw herself forward and managed to end her days. A hand clawing at the surface of the water, a muddied boot kicking up awkwardly, a bubble of skirt briefly floating—then she was gone. Ripples faded and the pond was still once more. The men cheered and moved on."

"And Beatrice and Virgil in all this?" Henry asked quietly.

"They neither moved nor made a sound the whole time and they remained unnoticed. As soon as the men dispersed, they fled the village. Images kept pressing upon them. Beatrice could see the face of one of the babies, the first one to be drowned, a fleeting, expressive pinkness, with a small escaped hand reaching up to its mother. Another face harried Virgil: that of a boy—he could not have been more than sixteen or seventeen years old. In his pursuit of the women, he slowed and kicked the ground in their direction, throwing up a cloud of dirt and pebbles, his kicking leg raised high in the air as he hopped on the other to a stop—this done with the easy, elastic vigour of youth, accompanied by a whoop and a holler. Then he started running after the women again. He was one of the loudest and most excited at the pond's edge."

"And he's the one they run into a few days later?"

"Yes, as I just read to you," the taxidermist replied.

"It's after they flee the village that Beatrice and Virgil come to the spot where they have the conversation about a pear?"

"That's right."

There was silence, that silence the taxidermist was so comfortable with, in person and in his writing, that silence in which things can grow or rot.

The taxidermist spoke first. "I need help with the games Virgil and Beatrice are going to play."

The words *games* and *play*—but said in the gloomiest voice and with the darkest expression. Henry felt a throb in his head.

"Tell me, the boy in your play—what happens to him after he kills Beatrice and Virgil? Is that covered in your allegory about animals?"

"No. I stay with the animals. I don't want games that need a board or dice or anything like that."

Henry remembered the story the taxidermist had sent him, "The Legend of Saint Julian Hospitator". Henry now understood the taxidermist's keen interest in the Flaubert story: Julian slaughters quantities of innocent animals, but it doesn't affect his salvation. The story offers redemption without remorse. That would be an attraction to a man who had something to hide.

The grocer across the street had got it right, Henry realized: a crazy old man. Sarah, in one glance, had got it right:

a creep. The waiter at the café had got it right. Why had he taken so long to see it? Here he was, rubbing shoulders with a stinking old Nazi collaborator, now casting himself as the great defender of the innocent. Take the dead and make them look good. How was that for murderous irrationalism neatly packaged and hidden? Taxidermy indeed. Henry now understood why all the animals in the showroom were so still: it was dread in the presence of the taxidermist. Henry shuddered. He wanted to wash his hands, his soul, of this man forever. He felt tainted by him.

Henry looked at the taxidermist. "I'm leaving," he said.

"Wait," the taxidermist replied.

"What for?" Henry snapped.

"Take my play with you." The taxidermist gathered the pages on the counter, seven or eight of them. "You can have the whole play." He went to his desk and hastily collected in his large hands all the pages lying on it. "Read it and tell me what you think."

"I don't want your play. Keep it," Henry said.

"Why not? It would help me."

"I don't want to help you."

"But I've been working on it for so long."

"I don't care."

Henry looked across the room at Beatrice and Virgil. He felt a pang of sadness. He wouldn't be seeing them again. Such lovely animals.

He turned back to the taxidermist because the man was stuffing pages from his play into the pockets of Henry's jacket. Henry grabbed the pages and slammed them onto the counter.

"I told you, I don't want your damn play. Here, have these too."

Henry took out the parts of the play he had brought with him and threw them down. The pages fluttered in the air and skittered across the floor.

"Well, in exchange, take this," the taxidermist said calmly.

He turned away momentarily. When he was facing Henry again, he had a short, blunt knife in his hand. He stabbed Henry. He wasn't even hurried about it. He looked at Henry, then drove the knife into his body, just below the ribs. It took Henry a moment to realize what had happened. The pain was briefly dulled by utter disbelief. The taxidermist stabbed him a second time, but instinctively Henry put his hands in the way and they took some of the thrust.

"What, what . . . ?" Henry puffed.

Henry could feel wetness beneath his shirt and there was blood all over his hands. Suddenly fear and pain shot through him electrically. A keening sound emerged from his mouth. Gripping the counter so as not to fall over, he turned and with leaden legs headed for the door of the workshop. He must have run, but it felt like a shuffle to him. With every beat of his heart his whole body was jolted and more blood poured out of him. He was petrified that the taxidermist would catch up with him and finish him off. The words "Sarah! Theo!" pulsed in his head.

He reached the door. In turning to go through, he caught a glimpse of the taxidermist. He was walking up behind him, his face passive, the red knife still in his hand.

Henry careened into the tigers and fell over. The pain ripping through his midriff was so intense and uncontrollable that he didn't so much get back onto his feet piecemeal as jerk himself up in one motion, as if he were a marionette pulled up by his strings. He made for the front door of the store as fast as he could. Would it be locked? The closer he got to the door, the more improbable it seemed that he would reach it. A hand would land on his shoulder. Worse, the taxidermist's blade would cut through his back.

Henry grappled with the doorknob. The door wasn't locked. It opened slowly and heavily. Henry threw himself out of the store and staggered across the pavement onto the street. Just then a car was approaching. He stood in front of it. The car braked and he collapsed onto its warm hood. Until then he may have been grunting. Now he was screaming as loudly as he could, though he was starting to snort and cough blood through his nose and mouth. The two women in the car came out, and when they saw the state he was in, they too started to scream. The man from the grocery store rushed out. Other people started appearing, alerted by the noise. Henry was surely safe now. Murder doesn't take place in the open, in front of so many witnesses, does it?

It was at that moment, as people blurrily crowded the edges of his vision, that Henry looked back at Okapi Taxidermy, still afraid the taxidermist might be following him. But he had stayed inside. The taxidermist was calmly looking out through the glass of the closed door, as if he were admiring the sunny day. Their eyes met. He smiled at Henry. It was a full smile that lit up his face. He had beautiful teeth. Henry barely recognized him. Was this the taxidermist's version of empty good cheer expressed in extremis? He turned and disappeared into his store, as if uninterested by the commotion at his doorstep. Henry collapsed, drowning in an internal sea of blood.

Even before the ambulance had arrived, the flames could be seen bursting out of Okapi Taxidermy. There was little the fire brigade could do. With that much wood and dry fur and so many flammable chemicals, the store burned quick and hard. A howling inferno.

With the taxidermist in it.

In a healthy individual, a broken bone that has healed properly is strongest where it was once broken. You have not lost any life, Henry told himself. You will still get your fair share of years. Yet the quality of his life changed. Once you've been struck by violence, you acquire companions that never leave you entirely: Suspicion, Fear, Anxiety, Despair, Joylessness. The natural smile is taken from you and the natural pleasures you once enjoyed lose their appeal. The city was ruined for Henry. Sarah, Theo and he would leave it soon. Only, where would they settle now?

Where would they find happiness? Where would he feel safe?

Henry regretted not having saved Beatrice and Virgil. He missed them with an ache that made itself felt even years later. It was the same kind of pain he felt when he had to be away for any length of time from Theo, a physical hunger for presence. He chided himself. Beatrice and Virgil, they didn't exist, not really; they were only characters in a play, animals at that, and dead ones. So what did that mean, *save them*? They were already lost by the time he had met them. But there it was: he missed them terribly. In his mind, he saw them as they stood in the taxidermist's workshop, Virgil so, Beatrice like this—he tried to make the pictures in his mind as clear as possible. But they faded, as memories of appearance always do.

All that remained now was their story, that incomplete story of waiting and fearing and hoping and talking. A love story, Henry concluded. Told by a madman whose mind he had never understood, but a love story nonetheless. Henry wished he had taken the taxidermist's play. That was another regret, that he had been so blinded by anger. But some stories are fated to be lost, at least in part.

Later on, on a few occasions, Henry looked at pictures of howler monkeys, nearly always photographed high up in tropical trees, but the evident wildness of the animals made it impossible for him to see anything of Virgil in them. Donkeys, on the other hand, were another matter. Once, at a

Christmas Nativity scene with live animals, as Henry got close to the donkey, it looked at him and, as if recognizing him, shook its head and twisted its ears and made a gentle snuffling sound. Of course, it was likely only hoping for a treat. Henry knew that in his mind. Nonetheless, under his breath, he said her name—"Beatrice!"—and tears welled up in his eyes. He could never again see a donkey without thinking of Beatrice and Virgil and feeling grief and misery.

After the stabbing, Henry went about remembering and writing down exactly what had happened to him. To help his memory, he read up on taxidermy. Any bit of information that struck him as familiar, he noted; that's how he re-assembled the essay the taxidermist had read to him. In a taxidermy magazine, he found an article on the taxidermist, with precious photos; these were the foundations for the mental reconstruction of Okapi Taxidermy. The essential part of the story, the taxidermist's play, was the most difficult to re-create. The sun of faith came before the generous wind, but which came first, the black cat or the three whispered jokes? The most elusive fragments on the sewing list were those the taxidermist had never discussed, such as the song, the food dish, the shirts with an arm missing, the porcelain shoes, the float in a parade. But bit by bit, painstakingly, Henry managed to reconstruct parts of the play.

At the hospital, as he was resting in his bed after the blood transfusions and the operation, the nurse presented him with a torn sheet of paper, crumpled and bloodied. She said it was Henry's, that he had brought it with him. Henry recognized what it was. As he turned after being stabbed, he must have laid a hand on the counter and unintentionally grabbed one of the pages from the taxidermist's play. Somewhere along the way, half of it had been torn off and lost.

Through a handprint of blood, the words coming through the red like dark bruises on skin, Henry read the sole surviving element of the play, a fragment to do with the body Beatrice and Virgil find near the tree:

```
Virgil:  We did what we could. We wrote to
         newspapers. We marched and we
         protested. We voted. After that,
         why not be cheerful? If we stop
         being cheerful, we give in to them.
Beatrice: Next to a dead body?
  Virgil: Let's give him a name. We'll call
          him Gustav. Yes, next to Gustav,
          for the sake of Gustav, let's play
          games.
Beatrice: Gustav?
  Virgil: Yes, games for Gustav.
```

Henry first gave to the story of his stabbing the title *A 20th-Century Shirt*. Then he changed it to *Henry the Taxidermist*. Finally he settled on a title that went to the heart of the encounter: *Beatrice and Virgil*. It was to Henry a factual account, a memoir. But while in the hospital, before he started writing *Beatrice and Virgil*, Henry wrote another text. He called it *Games for Gustav*. It was too short to be a novel, too disjointed to be a short story, too realistic to be a poem. Whatever it was, it was the first piece of fiction Henry had written in years.

Games for Gustav

GAME NUMBER ONE

Your ten-year-old son is speaking to you.
He says he has found a way of obtaining
some potatoes to feed your starving family.
If he is caught, he will be killed.
Do you let him go?

Game Number Two

You are a barber.

You are working in a room full of people.

You shear them and then they are led away and killed.

You do this all day, every day. A new group is brought in.

You recognize the wife and sister of a good friend.

They recognize you too, with joy in their eyes.

You embrace.

They ask you what is going to happen to them.

What do you tell them?

You are holding your granddaughter's hand.
Neither of you is well after the long trip
with no food or water.
Together, you are taken to the "infirmary" by a soldier.
The place turns out to be a pit where people are
being "cured with a single pill," as the soldier puts it,
that is, with a single shot to the back of the head.
The pit is full of bodies, some of them still moving.
There are six people ahead of you in the line.
Your granddaughter looks up at you
and asks you a question.
What is that question?

GAME NUMBER FOUR

An armed guard tells you to sing. You sing.
He tells you to dance. You dance.
He tells you to pretend you are a pig.
You pretend you are a pig.
He tells you to lick his boot. You lick his boot.
Then he tells you to "_____,"
and it's a foreign word you don't understand.
What action do you do?

GAME NUMBER FIVE

The order comes at gunpoint:
you and your family and all the people around you
must strip naked.
You are with your seventy-two-year-old father,
your sixty-eight-year-old mother,
your spouse, your sister, a cousin,
and your three children,
aged fifteen, twelve and eight.
After you have finished undressing,
where do you look?

GAME NUMBER SIX

You are about to die.

Next to you is a stranger. He turns to you.

He says something in a language you don't understand.

What do you do?

GAME NUMBER SEVEN

Your daughter is clearly dead.
If you step on her head, you can reach higher,
where the air is better.
Do you step on your daughter's head?

GAME NUMBER EIGHT

Afterwards, when it's all over, you are sad.

Your sadness is all-consuming and ever-present.

You want to escape it.

What do you do?

GAME NUMBER NINE

Afterwards, when it's all over, you meet God.
What do you say to God?

GAME NUMBER TEN

Afterwards, when it's all over, you overhear a joke.
At the punch line the listeners gasp,
bringing their hands to their mouths,
and then they roar with laughter.
The joke is about your suffering and your loss.
What is your reaction?

Of your community of 1,650 souls, 122 have survived.
You hear that your entire extended family is dead,
that your house has been taken over by strangers,
that all your possessions have been stolen.
You also hear that the new government wants to
turn a new page and address the errors of the past.
Do you return home?

GAME NUMBER TWELVE

A doctor is speaking to you:
"This pill will erase your memory.
You will forget all your suffering and all your loss.
But you will also forget your entire past."
Do you swallow the pill?

GAME NUMBER THIRTEEN

ABOUT THE AUTHOR

Born in Spain in 1963, Yann Martel studied philosophy at Trent University, worked at odd jobs—tree planter, dishwasher, security guard—and traveled widely before turning to writing. He is the author of the internationally acclaimed novel *Life of Pi*, which won the 2002 Man Booker Prize, was translated into forty-one languages, and spent over a year on the *New York Times* bestseller list. His collection of short stories, *The Facts Behind the Helsinki Roccamatios*, and his first novel, *Self*, both received critical acclaim. He has also published a collection of letters to the prime minister of Canada, *What Is Stephen Harper Reading?* Yann Martel lives in Saskatoon, Saskatchewan, with the writer Alice Kuipers and their son, Theo.

Yann Martel is available for select readings and lectures. To inquire about a possible appearance, please visit www.rhspeakers.com or call 212-572-2013.